**"Dam...** over her slender body.

"That dress has been driving me crazy all night. ...en dying to see you in the light."

...smiled and turned in a slow circle, lifting her arms behind her head. "Well, here I am."

In a flash Darius was across the room and had ...r wrapped in his arms. "And all night I've been thinking about taking it off you."

...mouth went to her neck, as he began removing ...e thin material with his teeth and sliding it down ...r body, kissing his way along the path he was ...ating.

...z felt as if her whole world was spinning on its ...s as he lifted her in his arms, carrying her to the ...d. "Wait! What about Dee and Marc?"

...s paused. "What about them?"

...t if they come in and hear us?" Liz was trying ...us, but it was hard when all his sun-gold skin ...eing revealed inch by beautiful inch.

...le spread across his face. "Then, I guess you're ...have to keep it down, huh?"

**Books by Elaine Overton**

Kimani Romance

*Fever*
*Daring Devotion*
*His Holiday Bride*
*Seducing the Matchmaker*
*Sugar Rush*
*His Perfect Match*

---

## ELAINE OVERTON

currently resides in the Detroit area with her son. She attended a local business college before entering the military and serving in the Gulf War.

She is an administrative assistant currently working for an automotive-industry supplier and is an active member of Romance Writers of America.

# Elaine Overton

# His PERFECT MATCH

KIMANI
ROMANCE

Be still, and know that I am God…
—*Psalms* 46:10

Thank You for always reminding me.

KIMANI PRESS™

ISBN-13: 978-0-373-86143-9

Recycling programs
for this product may
not exist in your area.

HIS PERFECT MATCH

www.kimanipress.com

Printed in U.S.A.

Dear Reader,

Thank you for taking the time to read *His Perfect Match*. I hope you enjoy Darius and Liz's story. Like fine wine, sometimes love needs time to age and evolve into something rich and wonderful. Darius and Liz discover this the hard way, but thankfully life gives them a second chance to get it right.

I love to hear from my readers, so feel free to write me at elaine@elaineoverton.com. I look forward to hearing what you think!

And make sure to look out for my next Kimani Romance title, *Miami Attraction,* coming out in April 2010.

Elaine

# Prologue

*Ten years earlier...*
*Cincinnati, Ohio*

As he stepped off the train Darius North listened to a voice mail introduction of his fiancée's cell phone before speaking. "Liz, it's me. I've been trying to reach you for two days. I need to talk to you. Call me as soon as you get this message." He started to hang up before adding. "I don't know why you're not returning my calls, but whatever it is I'm sure we can work through it, just call me. Okay?" He tucked the cell phone back into the case attached to his belt.

Slinging his tote bag over his shoulder he moved through the crowded train station and out to the main entrance where cabs waited for fares. His troubled mind was running in a thousand directions. Something was wrong. She was having second thoughts. Darius knew it as certain as he knew his own name. He could feel it.

He climbed into one of the available cabs.

"Where to?" the driver called over his shoulder.

Darius gave his home address and a few seconds later the car was in motion. He settled back in the seat knowing it would be at least twenty minutes before they reached his apartment complex.

He stared out the window at the passing cityscape as his problems raced through his mind. Whatever was going on with Liz had started over a month ago. She'd changed almost overnight. Now, if he said up—she said down. If he said left—she said right. He'd tried to talk to her before leaving on his trip and she'd just brushed him off.

Which was extremely unusual. Liz was the most agreeable person he knew. He thought back to the last getaway they'd had. He'd planned a romantic weekend retreat to a local medieval-style castle. She'd not even known where they were going until they had arrived, and the surprise on her face when they pulled up to the castle had been well worth the effort. They'd had a terrific time that weekend, but that was before all the wedding plans had begun.

At first, he'd assumed it was just the usual nervousness that came with getting married. After all, he was experiencing his own share of it. The idea of taking responsibility for the financial and emotional well-being of another human being was daunting to say the least.

But he was prepared. Probably more prepared than most twenty-four-year-old men. After all he had a successful business to provide for them. And not only was it successful but thriving.

At the age of eighteen, straight out of high school,

he'd signed up for the franchise-training program at the deli he worked in. Within a year, he was opening his own store. Two years later, another, and another across town, and now he was returning from a planning meeting in a city fifty miles away where he was preparing to open more delis and supermarkets.

Liz, a recent college graduate with a philosophy degree, could do much worse than him, he thought. So, what was her problem? His phone rang and he quickly answered it.

"Hey, man, where are you? I called the hotel you were staying at and they said you checked out."

"Hey, Darren. Yeah, I decided to come back a day early. What's up?"

There was a long pause before his brother finally said, "Nothing—nothing, just wanted to see if you needed any last-minute help with anything."

Darius frowned. "No, you just make sure you bring the ring."

"Of course."

His frown deepened. He loved his big brother, but Darren wasn't exactly the reliable type. "Did your tux arrive?"

"Um…yeah, about that."

Darius laughed, already knowing what his brother's complaint would be. "What about it?"

"It's green."

"Sage."

"What?"

"Sage. Liz picked the colors—not me."

"At the shop we tried on black tuxes."

"That was just for sizing. I thought I told you that?"

"You know damn well you didn't say anything about green tuxedos."

Darius laughed again. "Sorry, brother, but I'm just trying to make my new bride happy."

"Are you sure you can?"

Darius felt a chill of premonition run down his spine. "What's that supposed to mean?" He waited for several seconds but when no response came he prompted his brother again. "Darren, what the hell did you mean by that?"

Darren's only response was a grunt.

Darius instantly realized his brother knew more than he was saying. "Look, Darren, if you know something, say it."

"Nothing to say—I don't know anything."

"Then why did you say that?"

"Just messing with you. It was a joke. You're too sensitive. Chill."

Darius's eyes narrowed. His brother was lying. "Darren, as my brother I would expect you to tell me if you saw something or even heard something about Liz while I was away."

"Man, you're overreacting."

"Am I?"

"Look, I just called to see if you needed some help with the wedding stuff. Never mind."

Darius listened as the phone went dead on the other end before turning off his own. Darren knew something. Something he was obviously hesitant to share. That short conversation was just enough to confirm Darius's suspicions.

Before he could change his mind he leaned forward and knocked on the glass. "Instead, can you take me to 5682 Willard Avenue?"

The driver gave him a quick annoyed glance. "That's thirty minutes in the opposite direction."

"I know. I'll make it worth your while."

That seemed to appease the driver because as soon as he could find an appropriate place to turn around, he did, and headed back across town in the direction of Willard Avenue.

Thirty-five minutes later Darius was stepping out of the cab and paying the driver his fee and a fifty-dollar tip. The man nodded his satisfaction before pulling away.

Darius stood in the drive of the small family home belonging to the Donovans. Liz's compact car was sitting in the drive right behind her father's pickup truck.

He walked to the door and knocked. It was a warm June evening, so although he waited a few minutes and knocked again a couple of times, it was not an uncomfortable wait.

Finally, the door cracked partially and half a face topped with a couple of pink rollers appeared. "Darius? What are you doing here?"

"Evening, Mrs. Donovan. Sorry to disturb you so late. I was hoping to talk to Liz."

Marian Donovan closed the door to remove the chain and opened it wide. "I'm sure she's in bed already. Is something wrong?"

"Who is it, Marian?" A gruff male voice called from the top of the stairs.

"Sorry to wake you, Mr. Donovan, I was hoping to see Liz," Darius called up the stairs.

The stairs creaked as the large man descended. "Darius? What's wrong, son?"

Darius, starting to feel a little ridiculous for getting this couple out of their bed for nothing, tried to play down his concern. "No, nothing's wrong. I just wanted to speak to Liz for a few moments, if it's not too much trouble."

They gave each other a strange look before Marian announced, "I'll go wake her."

"Thank you." Darius called to her retreating back as she climbed the stairs.

"Come on in." Will Donovan gestured to the living room. "Have a seat."

The two men entered the small, cozily decorated room, and sat at opposite ends of the couch.

"You sure everything is okay, Darius?" Will asked, leaning forward to meet the younger man's eyes.

Darius tried to smile reassuringly. "Yes, sir. It's just that I haven't been able to reach her by phone for a couple of days." His smile widened to a grin. "Just want to make sure she hasn't changed her mind."

Will chuckled loudly. "Better not, considering the money me and her mama have spent on this little event." He reached over and patted Darius's shoulder. "Don't worry, son. She's probably just a little nervous. Perfectly natural."

"Yes, sir." Darius nodded obediently, and tried to tamp down his own concern as he watched Marian Donovan descend the stairs alone.

Her troubled eyes first went to her husband as both men stood to greet her. "She's not in her room."

Will frowned. "What do you mean she's not in her room?" He crossed the floor and pulled back the curtains on the windows facing the front of the house. "There's her car right there."

"I know. She must've gone out with some girlfriends after we went to bed." Darius did not miss the way his future mother-in-law avoided eye contact with him. "I

guess she's making the most of being a single woman."
Marian tried to laugh, but the sound sort of faded off
in a squeak.

Will's face was twisted in a harsh frown. "Without
even leaving a note?" He crossed the room and grabbed
the cordless phone from his base on a side table. He
quickly dialed his daughter's cell phone number.

Marian and Darius stood patiently, although Darius
was feeling anything but patient. His earlier concern had
deepened to an almost terrifying fear.

"Where the hell are you?" Will Donovan growled
into the phone. "Call home as soon as you get this
message, young lady!" He slammed the phone down on
the base and flopped down in the chair next to the table.
"Sorry, Darius. I don't know what's gotten into that girl
lately. This is the third time she's done this in the past
couple of weeks."

"Will!" Marian hissed.

He rolled his eyes at his wife and continued, unin-
timidated. "The man has a right to know, Marian."

Marian crossed to stand between her husband and
Darius. "It's just regular wedding jitters, Darius. Every-
body has them. I'm sure you're nervous in your own
way, as well."

Darius tried to force a smile. "Yes, ma'am. I'm a little
nervous. I'm going to head home." He turned toward the
front door, then paused and looked over his shoulder.
"Could you call me and let me know when she makes
it in? Just so I know she's okay."

Will simply nodded and Marian called out, "Of
course we'll call you. I'm sure she's just out with some
girlfriends."

*Or another man,* Darius thought. But the worried

expressions on both her parents' face let him know he was not the only one thinking it.

Just before five, Darius was awakened by a phone call from a tired-sounding Marian announcing that Liz had finally made it home.

"Can I speak to her?" he asked.

"Um, Darius, maybe now is not a good time. She just had a big argument with her father and I just don't think she's…"

"It's okay. I understand."

"Maybe you should just give her some time to herself. I really think she's just nervous about Saturday."

"Yeah, that's probably it."

"Okay, then, we'll see you at the church on Saturday."

But as he hung up the phone and laid back down, Darius realized he did *not* understand. Somehow, his well-planned-out life was becoming complicated; things were changing, and he did not understand at all.

Two days later, dressed in his sage-and-black tuxedo, Darius knocked on the door to the dressing room in the back of the church, and felt a sinking feeling in the pit of his stomach. "Liz? You in there?"

In the distance he could hear a piano solo of Jeffrey Osborne's "On the Wings of Love" coming from the sanctuary. One of Liz's friends, a bridesmaid, Kelly, hurried toward him down the hall, her sage-green gown lifted to her knees revealing white stockings with a severe tear down the left leg.

As she reached him, Darius asked, "Have you seen Liz this morning?"

She seemed distressed as she bobbed her head, the flowers threaded through her blond tresses weaving precariously. "Yes, about an hour ago." She gestured to the closed door. "She should still be in there. I was just coming to see if she had any extra stockings." She extended her leg. "Mine are ruined."

He knocked on the door again. "Liz?" He cracked the door a bit and the first thing he saw was Marian Donovan reflected in the full-length standing mirror on the other side of the room. She was reading something.

"Mrs. Donovan? Is Liz here?"

Marian Donovan swung around with a terrified expression on her face. "What? Oh, no, no—she's not." She rushed across the room to them. "Kelly, would you be a dear and go find my husband?"

Kelly's wide blue eyes looked nervously between Darius and Marian, and then she hurried away to find Will Donovan.

With a loud swallow, Marian finally looked directly at Darius. "Darius, come in here. We…we need to talk."

Darius started into the room on shaky legs. He knew. With absolute certainty he *knew* what he was about to be told.

Marian closed the door and handed him the note. "I found this a few minutes ago."

With clumsy fingers he unfolded the note and quickly scanned the scrawled writing.

Darius,
As much as it pains me to tell you in this manner, I cannot in good conscience go through with our wedding. I'm in love with someone else. I'm so sorry to hurt you this way, but to marry you would mean being untrue to my own heart…

He heard the door behind him burst open and Will Donovan's blustery voice in some kind of deep discussion or argument with his wife, Darius couldn't focus his mind enough to tell. Nor, did he care. He felt like he was in a fog, an agonizing, torturous fog.

He could hear others pouring into the room, his own parents' voices were mingled with the rest. But he was trying to see through the newly formed tears in his eyes to read the rest of the letter.

I hope you believe me when I tell you that I wish you only the best life has to offer and I hope, I truly hope that one day you can forgive us. I do love you, Darius, in my own way. But I have discovered too late that the love I feel for you is more that of a brother for a sister and not the deep emotional attachment I feel now.

Someone was sobbing, no…a couple of someones. And he felt a comforting hand on his shoulder.

Please don't look for me, go on with your life and find the happiness you deserve. And tell my parents I'm sorry, I never meant to hurt them, either.
Liz

Darius slowly folded the note closed exactly as he'd received it and turned to face the family and friends crowded into the small room.

His mother pushed her way forward and took his face between her hands. "Darius? Are you okay, baby?"

He nodded and closed his eyes tightly to hold back the tears. Not here. Not now.

Carol North hugged her eldest son to her, and then said, "I'll get your brother to drive you home." She looked around, but it was impossible to see anything in the mass of chattering people. "Darren! Darren where are you?"

No answer came for several seconds, so she turned to her husband, Jimmy, who'd worked his way to his son's side. "You know where Darren is?"

He shook his head. "Has anyone seen Darren?" He called over the crowd, but the incessant chatter continued and no one offered an answer.

Feeling his chest heave, Darius unfolded the note and reread ten words that were now taking on a new meaning. "I truly hope that one day you can forgive us."

*Us.*

Us?

Darius reached behind himself, and amazingly he found a chair to sit in before his legs finally gave way.

Carol worked her way over to the back of the chair and gently put her hands on his shoulders, as if by touch alone she could remove his pain. He could feel her turning her body in each direction still searching for her other son, the one she expected to help his brother now.

Darius could've told her Darren wasn't there. *Us.* By now, both his brother and his fiancée were long gone. On the way to their new life…together.

*Two months later…*
*Las Vegas, Nevada*

Elizabeth Donovan sat on the window seat of the small hotel room watching the bright-red neon sign of the strip club across the street flash its invitation of topless women. She pulled her knees to her chest, folded her arms across them and finally surrendered to the tears she'd fought for too long. What a complete mess she'd made of her life.

Her comfortable world filled with the safe haven of family and friends seemed to have disappeared before her very eyes. Some mornings she woke believing the past two months had been nothing more than a nightmare. Then she would sit up in the bed, look around the shabby little hotel room and remember. It was real. All of it. Every horrific detail. And she had no one to blame but herself.

How had everything gone so wrong, so fast? It seemed like years since she'd stood before the full-length mirror being fitted for her wedding gown, when in fact it had only been a few months. She'd been so sure of everything then, including what to expect of her future. Now, she wasn't sure of anything, not even her own mind.

Almost from the time they were children playing together, Liz had known and accepted that Darius North would always be a part of her life. Although he was five years older than she, her family had had no objections when they'd started dating four years ago. Even then Darius had a reputation as being an upstanding, dependable young man.

Over the years he'd proven to be everything it was assumed he would be. Respectful, generous-hearted, reliable. And the more he lived up to his stellar reputation, the more Liz accepted a secret truth in her heart that she would never admit aloud. For all his wonderful virtues, Darius nearly bored her to tears.

With Darius nothing was ever a surprise. Not even a surprise was a surprise. Every year on their anniversary when he handed her a gift-wrapped box Liz could guess what it was before opening it. Darius followed the traditional anniversary-gift guidelines as if it were gospel.

First year paper, second year cotton and so forth. In fact, Darius *always* followed the set guidelines. He never broke the rules, and she knew he never would.

At twenty-one, Liz already knew what her life would hold. She would marry Darius, the staid deli owner from Ohio, and they would probably have two, three children at the most. They would buy a small brick home in a Cincinnati suburb and continue to belong to their Methodist Church, Blessed Mary, where Darius would eventually become a deacon. Liz knew this because Darius had laid it all out to her some time ago. And Darius always did what he said he would. Always.

Using the back of her hand she carelessly wiped at her tear-filled eyes. What she wouldn't give to have that predictable man back in her life. But that particular bridge had been burnt to ash. There was no going back. Ever. All because of one man—no, that wasn't fair. It was as much her fault as it was Darren's.

Liz leaned her head against the window and sighed at the feel of the cool glass against her heated face. She glanced down at the thin white plastic stick resting in her limp hand. Through her blur of tears she could barely make out the pink strip in the tiny opening. It didn't matter. She'd already spent the past hour staring at it. No, there was no going back now.

Seeing a car pull up below she hastily wiped her eyes hoping it was someone dropping Darren off. She glanced at the clock and felt her heart sink a little more. It was just a little past midnight. Darren never made it back before dawn—on the mornings he bothered to come back at all.

The car door slammed shut and she was able to make out the Las Vegas Police Department symbol. For some reason she found herself focused on that symbol. It wasn't unusual to see LVPD pulling up in front of the hotel that also served as a halfway house. But there was something about the way the neon sign across the street flashed over the car that cast the symbol in a strange light.

She watched as the two uniformed officers entered the building below, and glanced back at the stick in her hand. Forcing her exhausted body into motion she stood and went into the bathroom to toss out the stick. She grabbed some toilet tissue and wiped the tears from her eyes.

There was no more time for self-pity. There were decisions to be made. Important decisions. And this time she would think it through instead of acting on impulse as she'd done two months ago.

This time she would make the right choices, because now her decision wasn't just for herself anymore. Just then, a knock came on the door.

Liz frowned as she headed to the door. She hesitated to answer, wondering who it could be. Darren was the only person who knew she was there and he had a key. She bit her bottom lip nervously wondering if one of the ex-convicts who occupied the building had been watching Darren come and go and knew she was there alone. She decided not to answer, until another knock came and with it a deep baritone voice announced, "Liz Donovan? Las Vegas police—we need to talk to you."

*Oh, God, what has Darren done?* Liz slowly moved toward the door and, after glancing out the peephole, she opened it. "I'm Liz Donovan."

Liz braced her body against the door to keep from falling down. She'd opened the door expecting to find two officers bent on doing their duty whatever that may be, and that's exactly what she found. But the sympathy in their eyes spoke volumes regarding exactly what type of duty they were required to do that night. In that moment Liz knew Darren would not be coming back that morning…or any other morning for that matter.

# Chapter 1

As the light white flakes fell steadily outside the window Liz studied the chessboard carefully, fully aware of the skill of her opponent. If she did not make the right move, he could easily have her queen in two. She glanced up at his serious face wondering what he was thinking. His thin, black brows crinkled in concentration. She knew he would show no mercy if she made a bad decision. She shifted her body, trying to get a look at the board from his direction, trying to think like him.

Her opponent released a heavy sigh of frustration.

She simply frowned at him, refusing to be pushed into the proverbial corner. She lifted her hand to move her pawn and thought better of it. She glanced at the king sitting on the side table by the hospital bed. He already had her king. She couldn't let him get her queen, as well.

*Lord knows, he'd never let me live it down.*

"Sometime today would be good," he grumbled.

"Don't rush me," she mumbled back. After a few seconds of consideration she slid her pawn one space to the left, and knew it was the wrong move as soon as a beautiful smile lit his face followed by the musical laughter she loved more than life.

"I can't believe you fell for that, Mom." He shifted his bishop to the right and swooped up her queen. What she thought he would do in two, he did in one. "Checkmate! I win—*again.*"

Nine-year-old Marc North bounced in the bed oblivious to the tubes running from his arms and chest to the nearby machines. "I win! You lose! I'm a winner! You're a loooossseeerrr!" He laughed loudly.

Liz simple watched the antics, trying to suppress her own grin. "And such a graceful winner at that." She knew in her heart that she would gladly lose a million chess games for that laughter. Although, there was no need to *try* to lose. Marc was exceptionally good at the game.

Ignoring her words, he poked his thumbs at his chest. "Winner." Then pointed both index fingers at his mother sitting across the board from him. "Loser!"

"You shouldn't call your mother a loser, Marc." A gravelly voice came from across the room.

"Hi, Aunt Dee," Marc was still grinning as his great-aunt came to the bed and wrapped him in a hug. "Mom lost—again. You'd think she would've learned by now."

"Learned what exactly?" Liz asked folding her arms across her chest, and accepting a light kiss on the cheek from her aunt.

"I'm the master! You'll *never* beat me."

"Marc." Delia frowned down at her nephew. "Your tone is disrespectful."

"That's okay, Aunt Dee." Liz smiled deviously. "There's more than one way to skin a cat—or a chess master."

Marc's playful smile disappeared. "Meaning?"

"Meaning, if your Xbox 360 ever goes missing—" Liz widened her eyes in a poor attempt to look innocent "—I don't know what happened to it."

"You wouldn't."

He looked so stricken Liz reached across the board and hugged him. "Of course not, I just wanted to bring you down a peg or two." She leaned back and looked at him. "Did it work?"

"Yes."

"Good." She stood up beside the bed. "You need to know that in the chess game of life…Mom *always* wins."

"That's because she cheats."

Just then a nurse appeared in the doorway. "Okay, Marc, the doctor's released you. See you Thursday," she said as she removed the needle from his arm and pushed the dialysis machine aside.

"Thanks!" With a leap Marc was out of bed and headed across the room to the chair that held his shoes and coat.

"Slow down, tiger." Liz rushed over to help him into his coat, ever mindful of his thin arms that she knew were sore where the needles for his dialysis were inserted twice a week, leaving them visibly bruised.

Marc crawled into the chair and waited patiently while his mother tied his sneakers. "Can we play in the snow when we get home?"

Liz's eyes widened as she glanced up at her aunt who

only shook her head in response. Given the draining procedure he'd just endured Liz could not imagine where he got the energy to want to play in the snow.

"Not today, sweetie." She stood and pulled on her heavy winter coat. "How about we rent a movie on the way home, instead?"

"No way," he called over his shoulder already headed for the doorway. "Tonight's wrestling night, right, Aunt Dee?"

"You got that right," Dee agreed, as the trio headed for the elevators.

"Alright, Aunt Dee, I'll meet you downstairs." Liz glanced down an adjoining hall.

She turned and headed down the hall, pulling on her winter knit cap as she spoke to the nurses she passed in the hall, realizing she knew them all by name. And why wouldn't she, considering how much time Marc spent in this ward?

Her bright, beautiful boy had spent over half his short life in and out of hospitals, and yet he managed to remain upbeat and optimistic. Most of the time. Sometimes the pain from the dialysis needles was so intense, even the most spirited people were brought to their knees. And Liz spent every treatment holding his hand and praying that God would somehow transfer the pain into her body instead of his.

As she approached the end of the hall she passed through a set of double doors leading to the intensive care unit. She paused at the last room and lifted her hand to knock on the open door announcing herself, but the scene that greeted her caused her to pause.

In the bed lay a girl not much older than Marc whose kidney's had completely failed. The only thing standing between the child and death were the various machines that did the work her failing body could not. The mother sat in a chair, her head resting on the side of the bed, and across the room the father and older sister stood looking out the window. No one noticed her standing in the door. They were all distracted by their own fears and concern. They were on a death watch.

Liz turned and quietly walked away without them ever knowing she'd been there. She had met the family through her juvenile diabetes support group, and knew of their daughter's recent change in condition. She'd wanted to offer some words of encouragement. To tell them it would be all right. But she knew in her heart it would not be. Their child was dying and there was nothing they could do about it.

*There but for the grace of God go I.* Liz felt a chill run down her spine as she approached the elevators once more. So far the dialysis treatments were working for Marc, but she knew all too well how quickly that could change.

Of course he was on the waiting list for a match, but so were thousands of others, many of whom had more common blood types than Marc's rare AB negative. They really only had one hope, one prayer and no idea of how or even if it would be answered.

As she stepped off the elevators on the ground level there were Marc and Dee on the other side of the large open entry in front of the glass revolving doors talking to Pete the security guard.

Even from across the lobby Liz could see Marc's wide smile as he chatted happily and knew he was bragging about his recent chess win against her.

She smiled to herself, remembering Marc's laughter

when he realized he'd won. Her only child was spoiled rotten, a poor loser, and she adored every inch of him. He was the sun in the sky, the axis of her world—and he knew it.

In her most ridiculous moments she wondered if maybe she loved him too much. She could not even imagine a world in which he did not exist and yet, thanks to his disease, such a world was a real possibility. She shook her head to remove the morbid thoughts.

"Hey, sexy lady," Pete said as she approached, and grinned, revealing several gaping holes between his teeth. *He has as many teeth missing as he has in his mouth,* Liz thought, but she would never say it aloud.

For all his useless flirting, Pete Daniels was a good guy and she would never intentionally hurt his feelings. Which is why she put up with his insistent come ons. They both knew he didn't stand a chance in hell, and yet he didn't let reality slow him down a bit.

"Hey, Pete, how are you?"

"Better now that I've seen you." He winked.

"I was just telling Pete about our game," Marc said with a smug smile.

"I bet you were," Liz answered.

Pete chuckled. "I'm surprised I didn't hear his crowing all the way down here."

She smiled, remembering she wasn't the only one who'd lost more than one game of chess to Marc. She and Marc had been forced to spend the Fourth of July weekend in the hospital, and Pete and his girlfriend Sal had smuggled in a holiday feast.

They'd spent the afternoon tearing through ribs, potato salad and corn on the cob, followed up by one of the best peach cobblers she'd ever tasted. The couple claimed it was their planned dinner and they were just sharing it with them. But the bland taste of the food immediately told Liz that Sal had cooked the meal just for Marc using very little salt and seasoning.

Realizing the time, Liz asked, "You're here kinda late, aren't you?"

Pete shrugged. "Yeah, pulling a double. My old lady is on the warpath about my spending habits, so I thought it best to stay out of sight until she cools down. Know what I mean?"

Dee tilted her head to the side with a frown. "What did you do this time?"

"What?" He shrugged again. "A man's gotta have his fun."

Liz knew from experience that Pete's idea of fun was spending half his check on lottery tickets. "How much, Pete?"

His eyes widened. "Damn. We've known each other too long."

"How much?"

He shrugged again. "Three-fifty."

Now Liz's eyes widened. "Three hundred and fifty dollars?!"

His lips twisted in a smirk. "Three fifty-four if you want to be exact."

She shook her head, and in a rash moment of generosity made an offer. "I'll lend you the money so you can go home, but this will have to be the last time."

Dee shot her a strange look, but said nothing.

He held up his hands. "No, no, I can't take any money from you." He shook his head insistently.

"It's just a loan."

"No way." He leaned across and placed his hand on

Marc's shoulder. "Look, you got real problems—and you need your money. No way could I take money from you. I wouldn't even be able to sleep at night."

Liz wanted to tell him that no amount of money could express her gratitude for his friendship and support over the years. Because of her frugal spending habits, the help from Aunt Dee and the medical benefits of her long-term substitute teaching job, Marc's medical expenses were mostly taken care of. But how did she say thank you for all the times Pete used his breaks to make special trips to the floor to tease and entertain the sick children there? Or the comic books he provided the unit faithfully from his own small paycheck? Those were just a few of the small things this man had done for them with no expectation of return and for that much kindness she would pay anything.

But Liz could tell by the determined glint of his eyes that this particular discussion was closed. And secretly she was glad for it. Although she would've given him the money, she really had none to spare.

Still she asked, "Are you sure?"

"Absolutely. Sal will cool off after a day or two."

"Or three," Dee said with a smirk.

Pete grinned, exposing his gaps. "Whenever, and then I'll be back in like Flynn. You'll see."

With a shake of her head, Liz turned to her family. "Did you guys forget it's wrestling night?" That reminder was all it took to get their little group headed toward the glass doors.

"See ya next time, Pete!" Marc waved as he headed out the door.

"All right, little man, and next time I want a rematch."

As Liz approached the valet station and offered the

ticket, her cell phone rang. With the city noises surrounding them, Liz covered one ear to better hear the caller. "Hello?"

"Ms. Donovan? This is Scott Banton."

Liz felt her heart skip a beat, and moved a few feet away from Dee and Marc. She swallowed hard. "Any news?"

Liz watched the driver pull her small sedan to the door, but even as her family climbed inside she stood frozen to her spot while soft white flakes fell around her. She was totally oblivious to the snow, as well as to the people moving around her as they entered and exited the hospital, going about their lives. She stood motionless as the winter cold filtered its way into her down coat.

She was waiting for the world to change. Waiting for a miracle to be offered. Waiting for the private detective she'd hired to give her the lifeline she so needed.

Finally the male voice on the other end of the phone spoke the words she desperately wanted to hear. "Yes. I found him."

*The Hawaiki Inn*
*Tairua, New Zealand*

Darius pasted on his best professional smile. "Congratulations." He handed the room key to the new groom. "I hope you both enjoy your stay."

The blushing bride was practically beaming with happiness and she gazed up at her new husband. "How can we not? This place is beautiful."

Just over the couples' shoulder was a floor-to-ceiling picture window that overlooked the Tairua Harbor. The turquoise-blue water almost matched the color of the cloudless blue sky exactly. In the distance the lush green mountainside of Paku volcano stood high in the middle of the perfect skyline. The palm trees swayed only slightly as a soft breeze rolled by and the bright sunlight warmed the hot-pink, soft lavender and bright-red tropical flowers indigenous to the area. Tairua was as close to paradise on earth as one could hope to get and yet Darius was certain the newlywed couple before him would probably never leave their room over the next two weeks.

As they turned from the counter heading up the stairs to their room, Darius returned to his task of entering invoices into the computer system when the phone rang. He answered on the second ring. "Hawaiki Inn—a little touch of paradise on the Coromandel Peninsula. How can I help you?"

A woman cleared her voice softly. "May I speak to Darius North."

"Speaking."

"Darius?"

"Yes."

There was such a long pause, Darius wondered if the caller had disconnected. "Hello?"

"Darius…this is Liz. Elizabeth."

His heart stopped for a moment, and then he realized it couldn't possibly be his Elizabeth. He struggled to find his voice. "Hello, Elizabeth, how can I help you?"

"Darius, it's me. Elizabeth Donovan."

His heart stopped once again, and, as if by some reflex reaction he slammed the phone down on the base. He took several deep breaths trying to control his breathing. *Liz Donovan?*

He walked around the check-in counter and took a seat on one of the plush tangerine-colored sofas scattered around the hotel lobby. Why would Liz Donovan be calling after all these years? How had she found him? What could she possibly want?

He leaned forward, bracing his elbows on his knees and cradled his head in his hands. *If you hadn't just slammed the phone down in her ear you might have been able to get answers to those questions, idiot.*

The ringing of the phone startled him and he glanced over at the desk. He sat still as stone listening to it ring and ring. After several rings it stopped and he released a sigh of relief. Then it started up again. He stood but found his feet rooted to the spot. After several rings it stopped again. Then it began again.

Just then, his assistant Alika came into the lobby and headed straight for the ringing phone, never noticing his boss standing a few feet away.

"Don't answer that." Darius's harsh tone cut through the air like a knife, and Alika stopped dead in his tracks.

His dark eyebrows rose in confusion. "We're no longer answering the phone?"

"Just don't answer it." With a quick glance at the confused man, Darius turned and headed out the glass sliding doors that led to the palm-tree-lined walkway that wound its way through the hotel bungalows and eventually down to the harbor.

Alika stood in stunned silence looking back and forth between the phone and the rapidly disappearing back of his normally super-composed boss. At first, he'd assumed Darius was headed back to his own bungalow, but then he watched him take the curve leading to the harbor. Alika prided himself on knowing his enigmatic boss better than anyone, and he knew he was going for a swim. He always swam when he had a difficult problem to solve. But what was troubling him now?

Alika glanced back at the phone when it suddenly stopped ringing, remembering the look of fear and anger on his boss's face. His natural curiosity ate at him as he tried to imagine what kind of telephone call could both intimidate and infuriate his boss?

With a shrug he turned and headed down the hall leading to the kitchen to talk to the chef. But just as he started to walk away the phone started to ring again. Instinctively he walked back and answered it.

"Hawaiki Inn—a little touch of paradise on the Coromandel Peninsula. How can I help you?"

"I'd like to schedule a reservation," the woman's voice on the other end said.

Alika quickly scheduled the reservation and, after ending the call, headed to the kitchen once again. His mind briefly fluttered back to Darius's strange behavior, but he quickly dismissed it, deciding that despite his great curiosity it really was none of his business.

## Chapter 2

"Are you sure about this?" Dee asked, sitting on the side of the bed as Liz packed her suitcase.

"What choice do I have?" Liz pulled several pairs of underwear from the drawer and tossed them into the bag. "He won't take my calls."

Dee lifted one of the well-worn pairs of underpants and frowned. "Is this the best you've got?"

"I'm not going there to seduce the man."

Dee looked directly at her for several long seconds. "Are you *sure* about that?"

Liz slammed the drawer closed. "How can you even suggest such a thing? My only child is dying—that I know *for sure!* This man is his best chance for a transplant—that I know *for sure!* Beyond that, Dee, I don't know a damn thing, *for sure.*" An uncomfortable silence fell over the pair until Liz released a deep sigh. "Sorry, didn't mean to snap."

"I know."

Liz moved on to digging around for shoes in the bottom of her closet.

"Do you think he'll do it?"

"Yes," she grumbled. "He'll do it."

She turned from the closet carrying two pairs of sensible flats in various shades of beige, and dropped them on top of everything else in the suitcase. She could tell by the way Dee was eyeing the case that her packing left something to be desired. But considering the stress she was working under she thought she was doing good just to get everything *inside* the suitcase.

Liz stood staring down at the hodge-podge of faded blouses and frayed jeans, trying desperately to ignore the feeling of fear building in her chest. "He'll say yes because it's the *responsible* thing to do."

Dee's eyes widened at the heavy sarcasm. She glanced back down at the open suitcase. "I know you're going there for Marc, but I really wish you would spend some of your savings on a decent wardrobe. You haven't seen Darius in almost ten years, you don't want to show up looking like a ragamuffin."

Liz braced her hands on her hips, and looked at the aunt whose advice she normally took as gospel. "Aunt Dee, I left him at the altar to run off with his brother. We haven't exchanged a glance or single word since then. Despite all that I'm about to show up at his place of business and ask him for a *kidney*. Trust me, Aunt Dee, there is nothing pretty underwear can do for this situation."

"It couldn't hurt," Dee grumbled.

Liz flashed her aunt a frown, realizing this was where Marc had picked up the annoying habit of mumbling under his breath. She began collecting her toiletries from the dresser.

"Besides, I need every dime for Marc's medical care—nothing else matters."

Dee walked over and laid her hands on Liz's shoulders. "That's not true. You matter."

The loud engine of a school bus grew closer and Liz knew that any second her son would come bursting through the door like a tiny dynamo. Instead of answering Dee's last remark she turned and headed to the front door to greet her son.

It was rare that she was able to greet him coming home from school, and watching his face light up as she opened the front door made it all the more special.

"Mom! What are you doing home so early?"

"I wanted to see you before I left. I'm going away for a week."

"Oh." His slender body, padded in winter gear, brushed past her and his heavy book bag was momentarily trapped between the doorjamb and Liz. With a wiggle and a push against his mother both boy and bag were soon hurrying down the hall to his bedroom. "Hi, Aunt Dee." Marc threw up his hand in greeting as he passed Liz's bedroom where Dee was quietly reorganizing the suitcase.

The older woman picked up a thin nightgown that had definitely seen better days and shook her head in resignation.

Liz, following him down the hall paused at her bedroom. "He doesn't seem the slightest bit fazed by the fact that I'm going away."

"Why would he be?" Dee asked, tossing aside a pair of frayed leather sandals she deemed beyond embarrassing.

"I've never spent a night away from him." Liz fought the sharp shooting pain in her chest that reflected her own fear of separation anxiety. "You'd think he would be a little nervous."

"Why? Because you are?" Dee shook her head. "Liz, all his life you've worked double time to make sure he felt safe and secure. And guess what? It worked. He knows you're coming back and he knows I'm here while you're gone. He's not nervous because he knows his world is stable."

"I guess you're right."

"I know I am. Now, go say goodbye before the cab gets here."

Liz came to Marc's bedroom and leaned against the door frame watching as he played video games. How to say goodbye? She was about to leave her son for the first time ever to fly around the world. She shook her head at the audaciousness of the task before her. But she would succeed. She had to. "I know you better not have any homework since you're playing video games." She folded her arms across her chest.

He shook his head, never taking his eyes from the television screen.

"None at all?"

The head shook again.

"Hmm…that's strange because it's Tuesday, and you always have a spelling test on Wednesday, so shouldn't you be studying for your test?"

He glanced over his shoulder with a frown. "That's not homework, Mom."

"No?"

"Uh-uh, that's just something the teacher tells you to do."

Liz frowned at his convoluted logic. "I have no idea why you think that makes a difference, so turn off that TV and get started studying."

With a heavy sigh he turned off the TV and turned to face his mom. "You gonna quiz me?"

"No, Aunt Dee will. My cab will be here soon." She came into the room and sat down beside him on the bed. "Marc, you know I love you, right?"

"Uh-huh."

"And I'll be back as soon as I can."

"I know."

"Do you want to know where I'm going?"

His young face became strangely sober. "I already know. Aunt Dee said you're going to see if you can find a kidney for me."

Liz's eyes widened. She wasn't sure how she felt about Dee sharing that with him, but it didn't seem to trouble him.

"Something like that. I promise I'll be back by Saturday."

"Okay. Aunt Dee said we're going to play hooky tomorrow and go to the zoo."

"Sounds like fun, wish I could come along."

"You can go with us next time."

"Liz, your cab is here," Dee called from the front of the small house.

"Be right there." She leaned forward and hugged Marc close. "I'm going to miss you so much, but I'll get back as soon as I can. I love you."

"Love you too, Mommy." He pecked her cheek and then, having done his duty, immediately began squirming to get free.

Liz slipped on her heavy winter coat and boots and,

taking the small suitcase from her bedroom, headed for the living room where Dee was peeking out the window.

She placed a soft kiss on Dee's shoulder. "Take care of my baby, Dee."

Dee looked her directly in the eyes as if to convey the sincerity of her next words. "You know I will."

Two and a half days later an exhausted Liz climbed the carpeted stairs leading to the welcome center of the Hawaiki Inn resort. Even in her bedraggled state Liz couldn't help but be impressed by the elegant bungalow-style hotel.

She'd arrived on the courtesy van along with six other guests and all the others had already gone in to register. But she'd just stood on the porch taking in her new surroundings.

Liz wasn't sure exactly what she expected but it certainly was not this warm and welcoming chocolate-colored wood-shingled village. Everything about the place said "Come inside my walls and rest." And after her long trip she was more than ready to comply. The problem was that somewhere inside those walls awaited the confrontation of a lifetime.

It had only been two days since she'd left the snowy streets of Columbus, but she could've traveled to another world. Where Columbus was experiencing one of the worst winters on record, New Zealand was just entering its summer season. Where Columbus was all freezing winds and dirty snow, New Zealand was a lush green landscape sprinkled with flowers and trees of every color.

The welcome center sat back from a cliff top. Standing on the long, circular porch gave Liz a breathtaking view of a harbor with the clearest blue water she'd ever seen in her life. It sparkled like a pool of tiny crystals in the bright sunlight.

Colorful flowers were scattered in pots and growing wild throughout the complex. So many of them she was certain she'd never even heard of before.

Unable to put off the inevitable any longer she entered the lobby and found it just as colorful as its surroundings. The large open room was decorated in tangerine and royal purple. Large, plush sofas were spread around beside small wood tables beneath walls decorated with abstract artwork. Candles, lanterns and tiki torches adorned the room. As she crossed to the counter the last couple from the van were getting their room key.

"Welcome to Tairua, can I have your name please?" The young Maori man at the counter gave her a wide smile.

Liz felt her spine relax and only then did she realize she had expected to see Darius standing behind the counter. "Thank you. It's Lisa Smith." She gave the alias she'd registered under, fearing Darius would cancel her reservation if she used her real name.

"Yes, Ms. Smith, I have you right here."

He punched something into the computer. "You will have the Nogomain bungalow."

"Nogomain?"

The young man smiled. "All of our bungalows are named after Polynesian gods and goddesses. Nogomain was an aborigine god that gave spirit children to mortal parents."

"Really?" Liz thought that maybe fate was sending her a positive sign given how desperately her mortal child needed some spiritual intervention. With impressive

speed the attendant explained to her all the hotel's ameni-
ties and gave her a small brochure to fill in the blanks.

A short while later, small suitcase in hand, she was wandering down the redbrick path that wound its way through
the collection of small bungalows looking for Nogomain.

A couple passed her looking so completely in love
that for a moment her heart ached for what she'd never
had. Further down the walkway she saw a group of teens
talking and laughing as they took the path that led down
to the harbor. And, as she spotted her bungalow and approached it, she noticed a group of people off to her left,
toasting their glasses. She placed the key in the lock of
the door, glanced at the group and felt her heart stop.

There in the middle of the small crowd stood Darius
looking like a Maori god himself. The years had changed
him, but she knew it was him without a doubt. His
perfect smile seemed even whiter. His light complexion
had darkened to a golden bronze. His short-cropped dark
hair had lightened to a sandy brown. *Funny, I'd always
thought his hair was black.*

That single thought reminded her of just how little
she knew about this man she was once engaged to. She
quietly moved from the walkway across the plush grass
to shield herself behind a nearby tree.

*Where did that body come from?* The Darius she remembered was lean and bordering on skinny. This man
was full of muscles—everywhere. From his impressive
pecs, over the six-pack abs to the thick thighs. If he'd
been fully dressed in one of the business suits he use to
wear constantly she would've wondered if anything was
padded, but wearing only swim trunks revealed that the
only thing padding his bulges and biceps was pure flesh.

She frowned. She didn't remember him looking this

good. She searched her memory and decided that was because he *didn't* used to look this good. Time had obviously been good to him. She fought down the slight resentment she felt, realizing that while she'd been struggling to put herself through school and at the same time take care of a sick child he'd been here living the life of a real-life beach boy. But justice wouldn't allow the resentment to simmer. Immediately her conscience asked the question: *and whose fault is that?*

She stood hidden behind the tree listening as he informed the group of guests about the evening's activities, including a full luau dinner. Apparently the Hawaiki Inn went to great lengths to keep their guests entertained.

It didn't take Liz long to realize there were changes other than his physical appearance. Darius had always been self-confident but there was a sternness about him that she'd never seen before. Despite the wide smile he gave his guests there was a hardness to him. Soft brown eyes that she remembered as being full of compassion were no longer tender. Now they were shrewd, analytical, as he scanned the group around him and sized up each individual.

For the first time Liz began to doubt her plan. She'd come to ask her ex-fiancé for the favor of a lifetime, but it appeared she'd arrived too late. It appeared that man no longer existed.

A few minutes later as she stood over her open suitcase preparing to unpack she was forced to admit Aunt Dee was right. Before she confronted Darius she would have to make a trip to the hotel gift shop and hope they had something in the way of clothing. There was no way she could approach the stranger she'd just encountered looking as defeated as she felt.

The old Darius would've taken pity on her and offered his help immediately. But the man she saw today would take one look at her lived-in linens and well-worn wools, realize she'd fallen on hard times and then proceed to eat her alive, all the while laughing at her temerity.

No, she was going to have to rethink her whole approach. She would have to exchange truth and desperation for cunning and manipulation. She closed up her suitcase and shoved it in the bottom of her closet all the while saying a silent prayer for strength and wisdom. Getting this new Darius to bend to her will was going to be a lot harder than she'd assumed.

# Chapter 3

"What you doing up here, boss? The guests are asking for you."

Darius turned at the sound of his assistant, Alika, coming up the brick stairs that led from the beach to the hotel. Darius stood leaning against the white wrought-iron fence that ran the length of the cliff surrounding the hotel. The sun was just beginning to set over the harbor, casting the entire valley in a soft reddish haze, and the gentle breeze added just the right touch to offset the surprisingly high evening temperature.

"Just catching my breath. Everything okay down there?" He nodded toward the beach where his guests were enjoying the luau dinner provided in first-class style by the hotel. It was one of the main attractions of his hotel and always a big hit with the guests. A small group of Maoris did a haka dance as the wait staff moved between the clusters of people serving dishes from various South-Pacific cultures.

When he'd first arrived on the island ten years ago Darius had been struck by the similarities between the cultures of the indigenous New Zealand Maori people, Australian aborigines and the Hawaiians. Having the same origins, much of their traditions were shared. When he opened his hotel he chose that shared culture as his theme.

"Yes, everything is going well. But some of the guests were wondering if you planned to appear tonight." Alika came and stood beside him. "I told them you would."

Darius smiled to himself. Alika was an excellent assistant and one of his most appealing characteristics was his ability to push without being seen as pushy. It was a skill that came in very handy with hard-to-please guests and tradesmen. Alika hadn't yet learned that his pushing-without-being-pushy technique didn't really work with his boss.

"Then it's going to be a little awkward when you go back and tell them I won't be appearing tonight."

"Why?"

"Well, because you've already told them I would be—"

"No, I mean why won't you? You always come to the weekly luau, at least you used to."

Darius continued to stare out over the bay, refusing to be baited into a discussion about his behavior over the past few days. He knew his entire staff had become aware of his dark mood, but until he figured out what it all meant himself, he had no intention of talking about it.

With one single, incomplete phone call his whole

world had been turned on end. He hadn't stopped thinking about Liz Donovan from the moment he'd hung up the phone. Why, after all these years, was she calling him? What could she possibly want? His eyes narrowed on the volcano in the distance but his mind was a million miles away.

For the past few days he'd been taking daily trips down memory lane reliving every painful moment in vivid detail. Instead of completing his payroll he'd spent hours remembering the night he'd proposed. At the time he'd seen only her sweet smile and the soft "yes" that rolled off her lips. In hindsight the hesitation in her eyes was revealed in stark contrast. He tried but failed to find the connection between her and Darren. What made them fall in love with one another? No matter how he searched his mind he could not find any evidence that caused that horrific conclusion to make sense. Nothing.

Every time he'd touched her she'd felt like his. Never once did he get any sense that he was sharing her with another man. Certainly not his own brother.

But Darren's betrayal was really no surprise. In fact, he should've suspected something was up when his brother became helpful. Darren had never helped anyone but himself. And in the end he'd helped himself to his brother's woman. Even his death seemed like providence. Killed in a Vegas club fight. Darius remembered his father once saying that Darren had been trying to die since the moment he was born.

Much to his embarrassment Darius's first question to his mother upon receiving the call of his death was about Liz. His mother had answered with what she knew, which was very little. As far as Liz's family was aware, she was fine. The unspoken message hung heavy between them.

He'd immediately understood that Liz's family had not gone to any trouble to verify her circumstances. It was assumed that since she was not with Darren when he died that she was fine. They didn't care one way or the other; she'd been cast out.

Considering how close she'd been to her parents that news should've brought him some satisfaction for his own suffering, but surprisingly it didn't. He didn't want to imagine her out there, alone, without even the support of her family. Despite everything he knew, some part of him would always wonder.

That was all so many years ago and Darius had thought he'd put it all behind him. Then, with one phone call she'd unearthed all that pain and anguish, and unfortunately his staff had bore the brunt of it. Over the past week he'd caught himself lashing out over the smallest infractions, and had even gone out of his way to avoid guests until today.

Somehow he had to find a way to repress the re-opened wound, but how could he when every ounce of his being was dying to know why she'd called in the first place? Until he had that question answered he would have no peace. She would stay with him every minute of every day. He would hear her voice in his hotel lobby, as he had that afternoon when he'd locked himself in his office determined to focus on the payroll. He glanced down at his guests on the beach…and saw a woman standing on his beach dressed in a coral halter-back sundress looking up at him.

"Who's that?"

Alika followed his nod. "Ms. Smith. She checked in today."

"Ms. Smith? Did she check in alone?"

Alika lifted an eyebrow noting his boss's interest in the pretty woman. "As a matter of fact, she did." He smiled. "She's very pretty, huh, boss?"

*Pretty* didn't begin to describe the vision watching him from the beach. Her shoulder-length black hair hung in a loose ponytail over one shoulder. She stood watching him with her eyes shielded by her small hand. The pose was strikingly sexy with her arm lifted, accentuating her slender body and small waist. Wrap-around sandals snaked up her elegant brown calves, making her wide-legged stance damn near erotic. But the tilt of her head revealed a bone structure that was engrained on his memory.

So many nights after they'd made love he'd lain awake simply outlining her jawbone with his finger. He'd always been fascinated by how the shape of a woman's small face could reveal both delicacy and strength. He'd thought Liz was that…delicacy and strength. In the end she turned out to be pure deceit.

He watched as the woman on the beach lowered her hand revealing her whole face and his mouth literally fell open. It had to be a trick of the lights. It had to be some tortured part of his psyche playing tricks on him. But as she smiled, he knew the truth for what it was. Only one woman in the universe had that smile.

She turned, exposing an expanse of flawless mocha skin, and started to walk toward the other end of the beach away from the luau and the hotel guests.

"Well, Alika, looks like you won't have to recant after all." He turned and headed down the brick steps leading to the beach, taking them two at a time, all the while keeping his eyes on the fast-moving coral-cloaked siren strolling away.

* * *

Liz concentrated on her breathing. *Stay calm. Stay calm.* But it was hard to stay calm when she was almost certain she was baiting a shark using herself as the chum.

With her head held high and her shoulders back she moved her hips seductively with every step, secretly wondering if maybe she was overdoing it a bit. She glanced back over her shoulder to where he'd gotten caught in the crowd of excited guests. It was working.

He was dressed in a loose-fitting, light-beige tunic that carried the hotel's name and emblem, safari shorts and open-toed sandals, and it struck her again just how different this man was from the one she'd known years ago. There was no way the Darius she'd known would've ever worn shorts of any kind, let alone shoes that exposed his toes.

She looked back again to see him gently but persistently pushing his way through the throng of people, never taking his eyes off her. She watched as he licked his lips and his eyes narrowed on her in an almost menacing fashion. *Okay, maybe it's working too well.*

She maneuvered her way around a grouping of inflatable balloon slides and bouncers where children played, oblivious to the darkening sky. She looked ahead at the empty beach that stretched before her. The sun was just disappearing beyond the horizon and the sky was quickly darkening. She stopped at the edge of the water, took off her sandals and waited for him to catch up.

Darius stopped a few feet away, still not convinced that what he was seeing was real. But it was her. Here, on his beach after all these years. How? Why? As he stepped closer, he realized she was more beautiful than he remembered, which seemed impossible considering he'd once thought of her as perfection in the flesh.

"What are you doing here?"

"I had to come. You wouldn't take my calls."

"Didn't that tell you something?"

"Yes. That I would have to come here and talk to you face to face."

"We have nothing to say to each other."

She turned to face him and he felt his heart skip a beat. "Actually, we have a lot to say to each other."

Looking into her warm brown eyes was like a homecoming. A sense of relief and satisfaction that he hadn't felt in years flowed through his entire being. The unfairness of it was almost staggering. How could she still make him feel this way after all these years? After all she'd done?

Her betrayal had almost destroyed him, and yet all he wanted to do now was go to her and take her in his arms as though nothing had changed. But it had. Everything had changed.

He couldn't do this. When he'd come down to the beach he'd thought he could have a reasonable conversation with her and find out what had brought her halfway around the world after all this time. He'd thought he could satisfy his curiosity and then send her packing.

Looking at the coral sundress clinging to her legs as the soft winds whipped around them he knew the evening was not going to play out like that. If he remained on this isolated portion of the beach, with her soft perfume wafting into his nose, looking at all that tempting bare skin, he would end up trying to satisfy more than his curiosity. And from the seductive way she was watching him he was almost sure his advances would be welcomed. *What the hell is she up to?*

"What do you want, Liz?"

"I need to ask a favor."

"Of me? Surely you're joking? Unless you're looking for directions to hell I'm not the one."

"That's where you're wrong." She moved to close the distance between them and Darius instantly stepped back. "You're the only one."

"What are you talking about?"

She turned back to the water. "Wow, this is even harder than I thought it would be." She chuckled. "And I thought it would be impossible."

"You should've followed your first thought. Because this is a colossal waste of your time and mine."

Outwardly agitated she swung back to face him. "You don't even know what I want!"

"It doesn't matter."

"I understand I'm the last person you'd volunteer to help, but—"

"If you understood that, then why are you here?"

"Just listen. I understand you hate me, but what I'm asking is not for me. It's for my son."

In that moment Darius wondered if his heart could stand any more shocks this night. "What did you say?"

"What I have to ask—I ask not for myself but for my son, Marc."

Darius felt as if his knees were going to buckle under the implication of that statement. *Her son. Darren's son.* The child that should've been his. Following her was a mistake. He knew that now.

"He's nine and—"

"Stop."

"He has diabetes. He was diagnosed when he was five."

"Stop!"

"The diabetes has eaten away at his kid—"

"I said shut up, damn you!" He turned and, taking long strides, headed back to the luau.

"He's dying!"

Darius stopped in his tracks, feeling his whole body stiffen from the tips of his toes to the hairs of his head.

"He's dying—he needs a kidney transplant. He has AB negative blood. I have O positive. I'm not a match. And he's been on the waiting list forever and there is no one. There just isn't anyone for him. The doctors say his very best chance is a blood relative. You would probably be a perfect match. Darius, you can save his life."

Despite the hostility radiating off the man, Liz moved closer to him and gently placed her hand on his shoulder. He flinched but didn't pull away and she took that as a good sign.

"I know I have no right to ask this of you, but here I am asking. Please, Darius, I'm begging you, please."

"I should've had security kick you out the minute I spotted you instead of following you here."

"But you didn't. And now that you know why I'm here can you in good conscience turn me away?"

He glared at her over his shoulder. "Don't you dare try to preach to me about good conscience."

Liz removed her hand and circled around to stand before him blocking his view of the luau. "If there was any other way, believe me, I would've chose it. My son is everything to me. I would do anything for him. I'd make a deal with Satan if it would save his life, so swallowing my pride and coming to you was small by comparison."

His brown eyes narrowed on her face in the same

analytical manner she'd seen earlier than day. "A deal with the devil, huh?" His full lips kicked up at the corner. "That sounds about right."

As hungry eyes roamed over every inch of her body Liz only then considered the lack of intelligence involved in luring a man who hated her to a deserted portion of beach. She glanced over her shoulder to be sure the hotel guests were within screaming distance.

She swallowed and determinedly pushed forward. "Will you do it?"

His eyes came up to hers and he simply stared unblinking while she waited for the verdict that would either condemn Marc or save his life. As he stared she felt her skin becoming covered in goose bumps, knowing her greatest fear was his immediate rebuff. Still, having no idea of what he would say, she never expected the next words that came out of his mouth.

"What's in it for me?"

She frowned, not sure she understood the question. "What?"

"Your Marc gets a new kidney, but what do I get?"

"Is this a joke?"

"No more of a joke than you asking."

She shook her head, realizing she'd failed. He was not only refusing to help, he'd decided to taunt her in the process. "If you're not going to do it just say so."

"I didn't say I wouldn't do it. But everything costs."

Liz focused on his face trying to determine if he was serious. She couldn't tell. "So what's your price?"

"Well." He thoughtfully rubbed his chin as if he didn't hold the weight of her world in his large hands. "The devil would require your soul. I can at least promise you my price will be much smaller." He huffed.

"Quite honestly, I'm not certain you have a soul to bargain with anyway."

Liz swallowed the sharp retort that immediately came to mind. He hadn't said no. She could stand any insult if it meant he'd do it. "So what now?"

He took a deep breath. "We go back and enjoy the rest of the evening. Get some sleep—if you can. And in the morning I'll tell you what I require in exchange for one of my kidneys."

She narrowed her eyes on his handsome face. "What the hell happened to you, Darius?"

"You did."

She bit her lip, knowing that was probably true. What she'd done could make a man hard and bitter. Was it really any surprise that he would keep her dangling miserably now that he could?

His eyes widened. "Of course, there is always a chance I won't be a match, and then any stipulations would be null and void."

"You'll be a match." She turned and headed back to the hotel.

He frowned at her retreating back. "What makes you so sure?"

"Because fate has a sick sense of humor."

# Chapter 4

After her tense conversation with Darius and his tentative agreement Liz found it impossible to enjoy the luau. She'd gone immediately to her room and called home to check on Marc. But it was too late, Dee said he was already sound asleep and Liz asked her not to wake him.

Without even the comfort of her son's voice Liz found it almost impossible to sleep, but finally, around midnight, the exhaustion of the long journey coupled with the stress of seeing Darius again overtook her and she fell into a deep slumber.

Darius spent most of the evening entertaining his guests—people from all parts of the world who had come for all different reasons. There were newly wedded couples and some celebrating anniversaries. There were students studying the plant life in the Coromandel Peninsula and local kiwis enjoying family reunions or just looking to get out of the city for a weekend.

Normally he loved the constant activity of managing a hotel, but tonight all he could think about was a woman in one of his bungalows. Never in a million lifetimes would he have imagined her arriving with her request. He tried to avoid thinking about Liz and Darren, but when it was unavoidable it was always in the frame of his memory. His twenty-two-year-old brother running off with his nineteen-year-old bride. He'd never considered what happened after that, especially since Darren had died so soon after they left together. Which meant the pregnancy was probably not even known at the time of his death. Which meant she'd gone through it alone, and had cared for a sick child alone. Maybe.

He took a glass of champagne from a passing waiter and downed it in one gulp. *Not damn likely,* he finally decided.

If there was one thing Liz Donovan knew how to do it was manipulate men. Hell, he was a prime example. Just look at the way the night had gone. She'd shown up in his hotel, his home, his domain, looking like a bright-pink lollipop ready for licking, and just when he was ready to stretch forth his tongue and take a swipe she'd dropped a bomb on his head.

As another waiter passed by he returned the first champagne glass and took another. She'd cornered him like a cat, a soft brown tabby cat and he was her favorite plaything. She'd played him ten years ago and she'd played him again tonight. He swallowed the champagne in two gulps. *Bitch.*

"Boss? Everything okay?" Ever-faithful Alika was instantly at his side.

"What do you mean?"

The young man let his eyes dart to the empty champagne glass. "You seem tense."

"Do I?"

In his peripheral vision he noticed Alika shake his head at the waiter headed in their direction and the man immediately veered in a different direction.

Pushing without being pushy, that was Alika.

He handed Alika his empty champagne glass knowing the wait staff would probably avoid him for the rest of the night. "Since you seem to have everything in hand, I'm going to bed."

"Good idea, boss, start fresh tomorrow."

He headed toward the stairs, speaking briefly with guests as he did so. No matter what else was happening in his life he would never allow the Hawaiki to be affected. This place had saved him. It had been his haven all those years ago, and he took great pride in its success.

His mind wandered as he meandered up the stairs. He had a nephew he hadn't even known existed. Despite how the news came, he couldn't help but find some joy in it. The boy was almost ten now, according to Liz. Climbing the stairs, he stopped in midstep. Ten? Was it possible? Could she have been pregnant when she ran away?

He shook off the thought and continued up the stairs. No, the boy wasn't his. She would've told him. That would've been the ultimate card of manipulation and she hadn't played it, which meant it didn't exist. He frowned as his mouth twisted in a snarl. Maybe she didn't know who the father was. *Bitch*.

He yawned as he started feeling the effects of the champagne. He stood at the top of the stairs for several long minutes thinking over the conversation, replaying every word. He'd known the moment she told him what she needed that he would do it. How could he not? But, he couldn't deny the fact that it felt good—really good—to watch her squirm for a while.

Maybe now she could understand just a little of what he'd felt standing in that church dressing room reading a letter left to explain the unexplainable. Maybe now she would understand what it felt like to have your heart ripped from your chest. How her one ruthless act had changed the entire trajectory of his life. Maybe she would, maybe she wouldn't. But before it was all said and done Liz Donovan *would* understand that actions bore consequences.

Liz wasn't sure what brought her out of her deep sleep, but the silhouetted man sitting on the side of her bed was enough to bring her fully awake. "Who the hell are you?"

She pulled the covers to her chest and scooted across the bed, her eyes trying desperately to see through the dark. Waking up in a strange hotel room had many disadvantages, one of which was disorientation. She had no idea where the door was, or even where her portable iron was. Either might be necessary depending on whether she would need to fight or run.

"I used to love to watch you sleep." The familiar but groggy voice came out of the shadows.

"Darius?" Her heartbeat slowed down only incrementally. She felt only slightly safer. "What are you doing here?"

"You're so beautiful, and when you sleep you look like an angel fallen to earth."

She squinted into the shadows. "Have you been drinking?"

He chuckled. "What? I have to be drunk to think

you're beautiful? I thought you had more self-esteem than that, Liz."

"What time is it? What are you doing here?"

"I don't know and…" He sighed. "I don't know."

"What do you want, Darius?"

"You can't figure that out?"

She pulled the covers closer. "Get out of my room!"

"Your room?"

"While I'm a guest here this is *my room*—get out!"

He stretched across the end of the bed resting his head on his forearm. "No."

She stood from the bed. "Why are you doing this?"

Even in the dim light she watched as his pupils dilated. "Nice gown." His eyes were glued to her breast where the thin worn material of the gown revealed much more than she realized. "Is that for my benefit? Are we still bargaining, Liz?"

Liz pulled the comforter from the bed and wrapped it around her body. "Why are you here, Darius? Is this to punish me some more?"

"Actually no. It should be. I should be back in my room thinking of all the ways to make you pay for this kidney you want so bad, but instead all I wanted to do was to be near you. Isn't that pathetic?"

She didn't answer and a quiet settled between them. She waited, hoping, praying he would leave but he didn't. Liz wrapped the orange comforter closer around her body and realized his steady breathing was slowing down. "Don't you dare fall asleep!" She shuffled over to the phone. "I'll call security!"

He rolled over to his back and folded his arms behind his head. "Good luck with that. I sign their paychecks, remember?"

"Quite the little dictatorship you have built for yourself here."

"Thank you. I'm happy with it."

"I'm not having sex with you, so you might as well leave now!"

"Who said I wanted to have sex with you?"

She frowned, slightly confused. "But you said—"

"What?"

"I figured…"

"That you were so damn irresistible I was overcome with passion and snuck in here to take advantage of you?"

"Something like that."

"Don't flatter yourself."

"Then what was all that talk about how beautiful I am?"

"You are. But in the right light so are black widows, wouldn't have sex with them either."

Ego deflated, Liz relaxed. In under five minutes he'd gone from calling her a fallen angel to a black widow. "If you don't want sex, why are you here?"

"I told you. I used to love to watch you sleep. Turns out, I still do."

Liz shook her head. Yep, he was drunk. She glanced at the clock and saw it was 3:04 a.m. "It is too damn early for this, Darius. Go to bed and I'll do the same."

"I've been thinking about our conversation earlier."

She stood quietly waiting, but he said nothing further so she prompted. "And?"

"Why didn't you try to reach me sooner? You said he was diagnosed at six and has been on the waiting list for over three years."

"I didn't know where to find you."

"My parents did."

"Your parents won't talk to me. Mine neither."

Silence fell over the room as they both retreated to their private thoughts.

Finally Liz broke it by continuing. "I hired a private detective a few months ago, and it took him a while but he found you and I called you as soon as he gave me the information."

"Who watches your son when you're away like this?"

"I've never *been* away like this, but my Aunt Dee lives with us."

Even in the dark she could see his wide smile. "How is Dee?"

"Contrary as ever."

"I remember her from when we were kids. Nice lady."

"She's been a godsend to me."

"I'm sure."

As another silence fell over the room, Liz realized she was probably not going to get rid of him anytime soon, so she took a seat on the opposite end of the bed.

After sitting in silence for several minutes she thought he'd fallen asleep and considered moving to the only chair in the room for the rest of the night. He startled her when he suddenly spoke.

"Liz…? Why Darren? Of all the men you could've chosen, why my brother?"

"Don't do this."

"I've asked myself that question a million times in a million different ways. I never found an answer."

"You don't want to dig up all this ancient history. It's over. It's done. We can't go back, let it go."

"Apparently it's not over. You're here. I'm here. I can feel your fear of me. It's almost palpable. And you have reason to fear. There were days I wanted to kill you with my bare hands. A part of me still wants to. So see? It's not so ancient history after all."

"What do you want me to say, Darius? I never wanted to hurt you. That was never my intention."

"Then what was your intention, Liz? Did you think you running off with my brother would make me deliriously happy?"

"I know I hurt you, but it wasn't deliberate."

"So you *accidentally* slept with my brother?"

"I make no excuses for my actions, Darius. All I ask is that you not punish my son for the sins of his mother."

"I have no intention of punishing my nephew." He flipped over and, before she realized it, his large hands wrapped around her ankle and dragged her beneath him. The speed of his motions immediately undermined her assumption that he was drunk. A drunk man could never move that fast.

Liz kicked recklessly but he used his heavy legs to pin her in place. Her arms flayed wildly looking for something to hit him with for all of a minute before he had her arms, too, pinned over her head.

Liz felt the first tendrils of panic not because of the vulnerable position she suddenly found herself in, but because of what she was beginning to feel. Feeling his heavy weight on top of her felt more right and natural than she could ever admit out loud. It had been so long since she'd held the weight of a man's body. The weight of *this man's* body.

And his smell. So many of those first nights in Vegas sitting alone in that shabby hotel room she'd closed her eyes trying to recall this very smell. She'd missed him more in those first couple of months than she'd ever missed another human being in her life. And being this close to him, having that familiar smell in her nose, and even with his additional muscle mass his body still seemed to mold to her own. It felt too good. Too right. She fought with every ounce of will not to wrap her legs around his waist to hold him closer.

"I would never punish an innocent little boy for the actions of his slut of a mother." He whispered in her ear. "No, I believe in holding the responsible party accountable."

"Get off of me," she hissed.

"God, you feel so good." Despite the strength with which he was holding her down, his soft lips touched her neck with feather lightness. "When you made love with Darren did you ever pretend it was me, Liz?"

"You son-of-a-bitch! Get off me!"

"No matter what other lies you told, I know you enjoyed our lovemaking. The way you melted in my arms was no lie."

"Get off or I'll scream!" She bucked hard, determined not to cry. Not here. Not now. And certainly *not* in front of this man.

Suddenly Darius was on his feet and she was free. "No need to be so dramatic."

Liz scooted to the opposite side before standing to put the bed between them. "Is this what you're into now, Darius?!"

Her eyes had adjusted to the dark and she saw his brown eyes almost twinkle with malicious intent. "I don't have to take what can be given."

She stopped herself from asking what he meant by that. She was afraid she already knew.

He turned and headed toward the door. "Meet me at eight for breakfast, and I'll tell you my price." He opened the door, paused and chuckled. "When you hear what I want you may wish you'd bargained with the devil instead." He walked out and closed the door behind him.

"I think I already do," Liz whispered to the empty room.

# Chapter 5

As she tossed one outfit after another across the bed Liz once again regretted ignoring Dee's suggestion that she buy some decent clothes for the trip. She finally settled on a navy-blue sheath with a gold chain belt and matching gold high-heeled sandals.

Spritzing her hair with moisturizer she brushed, twisted and pinned it in an upturned ponytail. In one day she'd already discovered that New Zealand mornings came in with scorching temperatures. As she applied a light coating of eye shadow and lipstick, she wondered why she was doing all this, and remembered the night before and the implied message in his words.

Staring at her image in the mirror she silently wondered if some part of her was inviting trouble. She glanced at the clock. She still had time to call Marc.

A few minutes later, fortified by her son's excited

words about their trip to the zoo, Liz left her bungalow heading to the main building where the hotel restaurant was located. Although Darius had not specified a location, she could only imagine that was where he wanted to meet her. As she entered the elegant glass-walled restaurant giving a spectacular circular view of the harbor, she discovered that when it came to Darius she would be wise to stop making assumptions.

She approached the hostess. "Excuse me, I'm supposed to meet Mr. North here this morning."

"You must be Ms. Smith." The hostess reached under her podium and pulled out a sealed envelope. "He left this for you."

Liz quickly opened the envelope and enclosed was a small piece of paper that read: Auta Fafine suite. She sighed and shook her head. Of course, they would meet in his suite if he planned to finish what he had started last night. And she had every belief that that would be his price.

She quickly found the suite and knocked on the door.

"Come in, it's open."

As she entered the suite she was immediately struck by the elegance of the place. The beautiful furnishings and artwork spoke of a wealth she had only guessed at until now. Darius had moved far beyond his delis and supermarkets of the past years.

This morning he was sporting a more corporate look, in sage-green linen slacks and an untucked, cream linen shirt. The clothes hung comfortably loose on his muscular frame, making him seem a lot less harmless than he was.

With his hands in his pockets, he stood watching her. "Good morning, Ms. *Smith*." He entered the room from the balcony. "I would've thought you'd be more creative with your alias."

"I was in a hurry. I just needed a name you wouldn't notice on the register." Liz closed the door behind her, still taking in her surroundings. "It worked, didn't it?"

"Yes, it did." He followed her eyes as she surveyed his home. "Just realizing you bet on the wrong horse?"

She straightened her shoulders and met his eyes across the room. They roamed over her body, taking in every detail of her appearance, and she found herself secretly satisfied that she'd taken the time to primp that morning. Despite her desperate need for his help, she was determined that he would detect no further weaknesses in her.

"So, name your price."

"Not so fast. Come, have breakfast with me." He gestured to the balcony.

She forced her feet to move and followed him out to the balcony where a small table was set for two with various breakfast entrees, everything from fresh fruit to danishes to eggs.

He held a chair for her to sit and she accepted the offer graciously until he bent forward and smelt her hair.

"Hmmm…still using that apple stuff after all these years."

She ignored the remark and opened her napkin across her lap. "Why don't you just get to it, Darius?"

He sat across from her with a wide grin. "Because the waiting is making you nuts."

"And making me nuts makes you happy?"

He shrugged. "Small satisfaction for what you did to me."

"And that's the ultimate goal here, isn't it? Punishing me for what I did to you?"

"Yes." He picked up a plate of fruit. "Try the kiwi, it's picked right here on the island. They are incredibly fresh and juicy."

She ignored the bowl of fruit. "Darius, I can't change the past and this…" She gestured around them. "This won't take away your hurt."

"I know that." He put down the bowl and looked directly into the eyes. "But you took so much from me, I just can't seem to help myself."

"What did I take from you, Darius? You seem to be doing just fine here. And I refuse to believe you've been celibate all these years. You could've married if you wanted to. I hurt you, I broke your heart—yes, but I didn't take anything from you."

His eyes narrowed and darkened at the same time. "You took my brother."

Liz swallowed hard, realizing for the first time that she'd only felt the tip of the iceberg in regards to the depth of this man's rage toward her.

"My last memory of him is what you two did. We never got the chance to make things right between us. I never got the chance to say goodbye. I knew Darren was selfish and deceitful but he was still my brother. I loved him, and now he's gone."

"Oh, my God." Her eyes widened. "You blame me for his death, don't you?"

"Shouldn't I?"

She shook her head frantically. "No, you don't understand—"

"What don't I understand, Liz? Darren was in Vegas with you. Because of you. He was working in that club to make money to take care of you. What don't I understand?"

Liz wanted to tell him the truth. That Darren's attraction to her had ended almost the moment she'd agreed to run away with him. That he'd practically abandoned her from the first day they arrived in Vegas. That she'd supported herself working as a cocktail waitress. That the only times she saw Darren in those last two months were when he needed a place to crash or to borrow money. She'd had no idea where he was or what he was doing most of the time, and whatever he was doing certainly was not for her. In fact, the only reason she'd stayed in Vegas, instead of returning home immediately to her family, had been the remnants of pride she still possessed at the time. But, in the end, after Darren's death and the loss of her job as a cocktail waitress, she'd been forced to surrender even that.

But she didn't tell him any of that. Somehow enduring his hatred and disdain seemed far easier than the possibility of seeing pity in his eyes. "Believe what you want, Darius. I'll say it again. I can't change the past."

He sat back in his chair. "No, you can't." He picked up a danish and toyed with it for a moment before returning it to the plate. "Tell me about my nephew."

"What do you want to know?"

"Everything. I've missed out on the first ten years of his life."

Liz let her mind wander to her son and couldn't stop the small smile that formed on her lips. "He's wonderful. Funny and smart, and terribly spoiled. He's an incredible chess player and knows it—did I mention he's a terrible winner?"

He smiled. "The North men have never been known for our grace."

"He's extremely lazy about his schoolwork and still

manages to get all As and Bs." She shook her head. "It's almost impossible trying to find an incentive to make him work harder when he does so well doing so little."

She looked down at the napkin in her lap and blinked rapidly, trying to push back the tears that had suddenly come to her eyes. "And he's the bravest person I know."

Once she had her tears under control she looked up at him. "The dialysis treatments...he has to have them twice a week, but he never complains, even though his little arms stay blue and purple all the time from the needles constantly being inserted and removed. The doctor tries to numb the area but I know he still feels the pain. He always tells me 'Don't worry, Mom. It's not that bad.' But I know it is." She blinked again, but this time it did no good and the tears welled up in her eyes. "I know it is. I can almost feel his pain. And when he's undergoing the treatment, he holds my hand and sometimes...sometimes, he squeezes my hand *so tight* and I know it's to keep from crying out."

Suddenly, Darius was kneeling beside her with his arm wrapped around her shoulders. "Shh. I'm sorry. I didn't mean to stir painful memories."

She used the napkin to wipe her eyes. "It's okay. My memories are not nearly as painful as his."

"He sounds like a remarkable boy."

"He is." She sniffled and wiped her running nose. "I always said he got the best of me and his father."

Suddenly the reassuring arm was gone, and Liz was surprised by how much she missed his warm strength. It had been so long since she'd leaned on anyone for support, the temptation to follow him and seek his comfort was almost overwhelming. But she remained in her chair. The care of her son was her burden and hers alone. She only needed one thing from this man, and then he would be out of their lives forever.

He returned to his seat and, resting his arms on the table, leaned forward. "I need to know something, Liz." He looked directly into her eyes. "Did you ever love me?"

Liz stared back, wondering how much of the truth she should share. He deserved to know that not only had she loved him, but she had never stopped. Even with all the pain vibrating in the air around them she knew beyond a doubt that she still loved this man. What a fool she'd been.

"Yes."

"When did you stop?"

"What do you expect to gain from this, Darius?"

"Some understanding of how I could've gotten everything so wrong. Where did I mess up?"

She frowned. "You didn't. You did nothing wrong, Darius." She twisted the napkin in her hands, wondering if she should share her next words, but before she could decide they were off her lips.

"I was such a coward back then. Too much of a coward to face you and tell you how I felt. I wasn't ready to be your wife, Darius. I wasn't ready to be *anyone's* wife. I was too immature, too unsure of myself. But I didn't understand that then, all I knew was that I felt like I was choking. The closer and closer we came to the actual wedding date—I felt I was suffocating."

"And what was Darren? Oxygen?"

She thought about that for a moment. "In a way, yes."

He stood and walked to the balcony bracing his hands against the stucco half wall. "I wondered if it was because he was younger, closer to your age."

"Maybe. I don't know. I just know he seemed…

exciting. Unpredictable and spontaneous. He'd been so many places and seen and done so many things."

"He dropped out of high school when he was sixteen, my father told him he would have to either find a job or get out. So he took off. We didn't hear from him for almost a year and he called to tell us he was working as a bouncer at a club on the French Riviera. *The French Riviera*—for goodness sake! To this day we have no idea how he got the money for a ticket to France."

"He told me about that." She smiled, remembering one of the few good memories she had of Darren. "He told me about all the places he'd been. He made it all seem like a great adventure." She glanced at Darius's stiff back. "I'd never had an adventure."

He huffed. "And you knew with me you probably never would."

"I know it's no excuse, but I was young and scared, and didn't know how to talk to you about what I was feeling. Darren offered me a way out—I took it."

He stood sentinel for several minutes just looking out over the harbor and Liz waited patiently, she knew he had more questions and he deserved answers.

Finally he asked. "Do your parents know about Marc?"

"Yes."

He turned to face her. "And they still wouldn't help you?"

She chuckled. "You obviously underestimate the importance of public appearance to the Donovans. I was officially an embarrassment. I and my bastard child didn't really fit into their country-club world."

"How did you survive?"

"I worked as a cocktail waitress and put myself through school." She sat up a little straighter, feeling pride in her accomplishments. "I'm a teacher. Kindergarten." She shrugged stiffly. "Although, I'm just substituting for now." She quickly glanced up at him and looked away. "It allows me more time with Marc."

Darius studied her face, trying to see what was not being said. Despite her fine appearance—and she did look fine, he thought, taking in the sleeveless dress—she could not be making that much as a substitute teacher.

He watched her discreetly wring her hands on her lap.

"Kindergarten, huh?" His eyes widened with exaggeration, trying to recapture the easy mood of the past moments. "Yikes."

She laughed. "I know. But they're not so bad, you just have to keep their minds engaged. They're so bright and hungry for knowledge at that age. I love my job."

He returned the smile. "I can see that."

In that brief moment, she saw a glimpse of the old Darius. The one she'd known as a young woman. The one she'd expected to find here. Warm, caring, thoughtful and an attentive listener. But it was only for a brief moment, and then he was gone. Replaced by the cold, calculating man she'd met on the beach last night.

"I guess you're eager to return home, huh? When are you leaving?"

She licked her lips nervously. "I guess that depends on you."

A mischievous grin came to his face. "You think you know what I want, don't you?"

"I think so."

He leaned his large body back against the stucco wall and crossed his ankles and arms. His eyes darted to the top of her cleavage, slightly exposed by the thin sheath dress. "Not quite."

"No?"

"No." He walked over to the table until he was standing directly beside her and, looking down at her, he said, "You're right that we can never relive the past, but I think we can recreate parts of it."

"What do you mean?"

He reached forward and took her hand, pulling her to her feet. She didn't know what he was planning, but the thought of saying no to anything was not an option. Her son's life was worth far more than her pride.

"When you hired your private detective to find me, did you tell him to look here first?" He walked her over to the balcony.

"No, why would I?" She stood beside him overlooking the harbor. The sparkling blue water of the bay was already sprinkled with swimmers and fishermen in small boats. The bright-yellow sun was high in the sky and it was turning out to be another perfect day in paradise.

She glanced at him and was stunned by the hurt look in his eyes.

"Our honeymoon plans."

"Darius, we never discussed plans, remember? You made all the arrangements." She quickly looked away. "You never asked for my input."

His face twisted in a confused expression. "Seriously?"

"Not even once."

He turned to face the harbor as a thoughtful silence settled between them. Finally, he said, "Well, this was it." He gestured to the surrounding areas. "After you left, all I wanted to do was get as far away from Ohio as I could. So, I decided to use one of the tickets and take a vacation. But once I got here I didn't want to leave." He shook his head. "It amazes me that anyone leaves this place."

"It is beautiful."

"It would've been the perfect honeymoon spot for us." He walked back to the table and picked a single plump grape from a bunch. "It still will be."

She turned to face him. "What's that supposed to mean?"

He looked up at her with a wide smile, but it didn't fool her for a single minute. His eyes were filled with pure malice. "That's my price."

"I don't understand."

He chuckled. "Yes, you do. Even though you don't want to." He popped the grape in his mouth, chewed and quickly swallowed. "Okay, if you insist, I'll lay it all out for you."

He took another grape and just toyed with it between his fingers. "First we take care of Marc. Once the surgery is complete and he is well on his way to recovery, you will come back here with me. For…" He tilted his head as if considering. "Let's see…our original honeymoon was scheduled for two weeks. So, just to show you I do have some compassion, I'll only require one week of you. Seven days—here with me."

She arched an eyebrow. "Doing what?"

His smile turned to a grin. "I'll think of something."

She stood straighter, needing to know the answer to the unspoken question. "Is sex involved?"

His grin disappeared. "Not against your will."

He popped the grape in his mouth, chewed and swallowed. "I know I'm not your preferred North brother, but who knows? Maybe you can make love to me and pretend I'm Darren. Would you like that?"

Her eyes narrowed. "Would you?"

His eyes roamed over her body once more in that

analytical way of his. "At this point, I just might take it anyway I can get it."

He moved around the table and rejoined her at the balcony and suddenly the air between them seemed electric with possibility. "So, do we have a deal?"

She turned her head to look at him. "Do I have a choice?"

"No." Instead of the supreme satisfaction she expected to see on his face there was something closer to resignation. "But neither do I."

# Chapter 6

Two and a half weeks later the only sounds heard in the waiting room of the second-floor nursing unit of the Cleveland Clinic were coming from the television set as a Minneapolis police officer won the grand prize on *Jeopardy*.

The three people waiting in the room were too tense even to speak or look at one another. Liz sat with her arms folded in her lap, rocking and silently praying, Dee sat nearby, knitting with the speed of some crazed weaver. Liz had no idea what her aunt was knitting, but whatever it was, it was going to be huge. A few feet away Darius paced relentlessly back and forth across the length of the room.

They were waiting for the final test that would confirm Darius's compatibility to Marc. Liz knew the chances of their matching should've been as good as humanly possible. They'd already crossed the first two hurdles by confirming that Darius did indeed have the rare AB negative blood type. The tissue matching had come back with good results, as well. Now they were waiting for the final test, the cross-matching, which would indicate the likelihood of Marc's body accepting the donor kidney.

Liz stood to stretch her legs and the movement brought everything else to a grinding halt. Dee stopped knitting in midstitch, and Darius stopped where he stood in the middle of the room.

"You okay?" He frowned, coming toward her.

She nodded. "I'm fine. Just stretching." Wrapping her arms around her body she moved away from him, walking over to the window to stare down on the busy city.

He came up beside her. "This is just a formality. We both know I'm going to match, the blood was the hard part, right?"

She smiled at his attempted reassurance. "Right."

She glanced at his profile once again, struck by the difference in his demeanor. It was almost as if just being back in Ohio had transformed him back into the man he used to be. The Darius of her youth. She'd noticed the change in him from the minute she picked him up at the Columbus airport a week ago.

Feeling obligated to play the hostess, she'd offered him her couch, but he'd surprised her with his denial, explaining he already had a hotel reservation and car rental scheduled. She'd offered to reimburse him for his costs, but he had been insistent in his refusal. And most shocking of all, he'd been a perfect gentleman the whole while, never giving any reminders or indication of their agreement even on those rare occasions when they found themselves alone.

Movement at the door caused them both to turn. Liz took a deep breath as Marc's surgeon, Dr. Feinstein, came into the room. The young doctor's face spread in a wide grin. "I have good news."

That was all Liz heard before the buzzing in her ears took over. She felt her legs go weak and reached for the nearest chair. Darius and Dee had both crowded around the doctor to hear the rest of his report. But for Liz the doctor's good news released the floodgates of stress and pressure built up over the past several years.

She leaned forward, resting her forehead in her hands. She felt a warm hand on her shoulder. "Hey? You sure you okay?" a deep voice whispered near her ear.

Liz shook her head and let the tears flow freely through her fingers. She'd cried more in the past month than she had in the past three years, but having so much of the heaviness that had weighed on her heart and mind for so long seemingly lifted all at once, the emotional impact caught her completely unprepared.

Accepting her nod, Darius continued. "The doctor wants to schedule the surgery for next Tuesday. You okay with that?"

She nodded again, knowing any statement she tried to form giving her current state would probably only concern him more.

"All right, I'll make the arrangements. Then we'll get Marc and Dee and we'll all go out to celebrate—sound good?" She nodded again and felt him move away.

An hour later, Liz followed slowly behind the group of new best buds in front of her as they worked their way through the crowded mall. Darius had instantly won over her aunt and son, and over the past couple of weeks the threesome had become almost inseparable. With them he was the old Darius, all charm and sweetness, and she couldn't help wondering where the surly man from Tairua was.

These two had no idea that man even existed, but she did. She couldn't afford to forget, and she didn't particularly trust this little metamorphosis of his either.

During the day, while Marc and she were in school, he ran errands with Dee. In the evenings he showed up for dinner and a nightly game of chess with Marc, in which the two worthy opponents were equal in the number of games won and lost. And even on those rare occasions when they found themselves alone, he gave her nothing more than an occasional wink and a smile.

Now she watched his broad back as he walked along chattering with her aunt and son, all three hand-in-hand. No, she didn't trust him. After all, this was still the man who demanded a high price for his precious kidney, and she wasn't foolish enough to believe he wouldn't collect.

As if sensing her thoughts, Darius glanced back over his shoulder at her. "Better pick up the pace, Liz, or we're gonna be late for the movie."

Following his lead, Marc looked back as well. "Yeah, Mom, hurry up! We're gonna be late!"

She smiled and moved closed to the group, but still kept a little distance, enough to see every facial expression when Darius looked at her son. And she watched him like a mother hawk protecting her chick. Always she watched, whenever they were together, looking for even the vaguest sign of recognition.

Of course, she had no idea what she would do if Darius ever did take notice of the fact that their profiles were exactly the same. Or that her son's exotic features reflected his Asian heritage. Darius's grandmother was Vietnamese.

Logic told her he had probably already noted these things and attributed them to the belief that this was his nephew. But logic be damned, she still watched him.

When she'd arrived in Tairua almost a month ago, she had been unsure of what to tell him about Marc. But one look into his cold, calculating eyes and the truth had died on her lips. The old Darius might've cared. The new Darius would only find a way to use it against her. And despite his good behavior over the past weeks, she didn't doubt the new Darius was still the soul of the man. Childhood had created the man she was to marry, the trials of life had created the man he was today. And despite their shared childhood, everyone knew there was no better teacher than life.

They reached the theatre box office and Darius paid for the tickets, then it was on to the snacks counter where she found herself in a tradeoff negotiation with Marc involving Nachos and Sugar Babies.

They settled on the Nachos, but as they were leaving the counter, in her peripheral vision she saw Darius purchasing the Sugar Babies. She thought he meant well, but she was going to have to talk to him about the rules when it came to Marc's diet. She knew he probably had very little knowledge of what life was like for a diabetic person, especially one with bad kidneys.

The action movie was everything the trailers had promised and, as they finished up dinner at home later that night, Marc was still talking about it and reenacting parts of it. Thanks to the movie they'd arrived home a lot later that usual, so Liz regretfully informed Bobby Fischer and Bobby Fischer, Jr., that there would be no chess tournament tonight.

Both males accepted her verdict with stoic resignation, but when she announced it was bath time that all changed drastically. Marc put up the fight of a lifetime, arguing to the point where she thought she was going to have to *old school* on his little hindquarters. But one stern "Marc," from Darius accompanied by *the look* and away he went.

Later as she stood at the sink rinsing dishes and placing them in the dishwasher Liz wondered whether she should have said something to stop Darius's interference. She finally decided that since this was probably the only time Marc would ever get to spend with his father she could afford to take a temporary back seat as the sole disciplinarian.

Darius came into the kitchen carrying the remaining dinner plates. "What a day, huh?"

"Yes. A beautiful day." She wiped her hands on a nearby towel. "Darius, I don't think there are words to tell you how grateful I am for what you're doing."

"No words are necessary, Liz. I only wish you'd come to me sooner." He frowned at her. "You have no idea how much I wish you had come to me sooner."

There was a questioning look in his eyes that made her slightly uncomfortable so she returned to the task of dishwashing as she continued talking. "I still feel like I should pay your expenses. You wouldn't be here if it wasn't for us."

"That's okay, I've told you a million times. I can afford it. And getting to know Marc has made it all worthwhile. You were right, he's pretty terrific."

"Terrifically spoiled."

"Rotten to the core." He laughed. "What the hell were you thinking?"

"That he was too adorable to deny anything to."

"Sucker."

She just laughed. He was right. When it came to her son she was a complete sap.

Just then Marc came bounding into the kitchen dressed for bed. "Do I have to go to bed right now?" He looked up at his mother with pleading brown eyes.

"Yes!" Darius announced swooping the boy up in his strong arms.

This was the fourth straight night he'd put Marc to bed, and once again Liz forced herself to stand by and allow Darius to do her job. But the sound of Marc's laughter as he was tickled all the way to his bedroom softened the blow. She could've never lifted him like that.

She finished up the dishes and started the washer before rejoining Dee in the living room.

Dee glanced up from her crossword puzzle. "Where's Darius?"

"Putting Marc to bed." She flopped down on the couch, feeling lighter than she had in years. "This time next week my baby will have a good kidney and be on his way to a normal, healthy life. Can you believe it, Dee? Finally, after all this time?"

"It is hard to believe, but so sweet to imagine."

"Well we won't have to imagine it anymore."

Dee gave her a wicked grin. "So, what are you going to do with all those extra hours you won't have to spend with Marc in dialysis?"

"What do you mean?"

"Well, you'll have more time for yourself."

"I'm still a single mother, Dee. We're not allowed time to ourselves. Didn't you read the rule book?"

Dee looked around the side of her chair to be sure they were still alone before leaning toward Liz to whisper, "I heard Darius on the phone a few days ago telling someone that he would probably be staying in the States longer than he'd originally planned."

"So?" Liz knew where her aunt was going with this, and she wasn't about to guide the way there. "You forget he's from here. His family is in Cincinnati, he probably plans to spend a few days visiting with them. That's perfectly natural considering how far away he lives."

Dee frowned at having her suggestion thwarted so easily. "You don't know that." She sat back in her chair and refocused on her puzzle.

Liz hid her smile, knowing her aunt would love nothing more than to see romance develop between her and Darius. But that was because Dee had no inclination of the kind of rage and hatred Darius was carrying in his heart. He might have claimed seven days in paradise with her as payment for his life-giving act, but after that she knew he would have no problem tossing her away.

Liz didn't believe for a moment his demand had anything to do with the warmer emotions. No, Darius wanted her for one reason only. He had a score to settle.

Shaking off the troubling thoughts, she forced herself to focus on the good that had come out of all this. Soon Marc would have his desperately needed kidney, and although she would have to pay the devil his due—for what she was getting out of the bargain, the price was more than fair.

She picked up the TV guide and the remote. "What's on tonight?"

"No wrestling," Dee grumbled. "That's all I know."

Meanwhile, in another room, Darius sat on the floor beside Marc's bed using words to paint the most vivid pictures imaginable. "The water is so blue you can stand on the shore and see the dolphins swimming beneath it."

"There are dolphins there?"

"Oh, absolutely. New Zealand is one of dolphins' favorite places in the world."

"Really? Can I see a dolphin?"

"I will make sure you see a dolphin."

Marc yawned and rolled away from his guest. "Night, Uncle Darius."

Knowing he'd just been dismissed, Darius stood from the floor. "Night, little man."

"I can't wait to go to New Zealand." Marc's words faded to where Zealand sounded like "Zeen."

Darius stood perfectly still, waiting to be certain the child was completely asleep before reaching forward and lifting the bottom of his pajama top to reveal the small birthmark on his lower back.

He sighed in relief. He'd first seen the mark simply by chance the first night he'd tucked Marc in. The boy had been crawling across the bed and his shirt rose with his body movement. At first Darius had been dazed, not believing what he was seeing. But he'd checked for the mark every night since and it was still there.

He placed a gentle kiss on the mark and tucked the covers back around the small body. And he just stood there looking down at his son. *His son.*

From the moment he'd met Marc he'd immediately recognized the similarities. How could he not? It was like looking in a mirror, except that Marc seemed to take after Nanna, his maternal grandmother, more than he did. He'd originally just assumed such similarities were to be expected. After all, the child was his nephew. His brother's child. And he was perfectly aware that he and

Darren did indeed look a lot alike. They had many shared features and characteristics. But the birthmark on his lower back was not one of them. That was his and his alone. As far as he knew no one in his family had ever been born with that mark before. Except now…his *son* bore it as well.

. It had taken every ounce of his self control over the past few days not to lash out at Liz for keeping this from him. How dare she? What was she thinking? He felt his hands forming fists as he fought down the anger building in his chest every time he thought about it. He took a deep breath and relaxed both hands.

He knew what she was thinking. She was thinking that he would never find out. And if it hadn't been for tucking Marc in that night and happening to see the birthmark, he probably wouldn't have.

He glanced around the blue-painted bedroom, decorated in primary colors and a rainbow mural that took up one whole wall, the bright-red race car bed with matching dresser and chest, and several toyboxes overflowing with every toy a boy could want. On the opposite side of the room sat a large TV with so many contraptions attached to it, he thought the child must have every video game system in creation.

This one room was in stark contrast to the rest of the little house. The living room had beige lumpy furniture that had definitely seen better days. The chair cushions in the dining room were losing their filling. The kitchen was neat and clean but the cabinets were sparsely filled with dishes and cookware. And Liz's bedroom was the saddest of all, containing a full-size bed and one battered dresser. He hadn't been to the basement where Dee had taken up residence, but he could only imagine it wasn't much better.

After participating in the testing over the past week it was no great mystery to understand where her money went. Hospital bills, lab tests and medications were all costing a fortune, and, despite her good medical benefits and modest lifestyle, she was probably still drowning in debt.

On the island he'd been given the impression she was living in comfort. This wasn't comfort. This was barely getting by. Why hadn't she come to him sooner?

He finally decided to hell with the whys, he was here now. And he would not allow her to keep him away from his son ever again. His eyes narrowed as he considered how discreet she'd been up until now. No, not discreet—sneaky. Maybe he should talk to a lawyer…just in case she decided to be unreasonable.

"Everything okay?" Liz's soft voice from the hallway startled him, and he turned to see her.

"He's out cold." He moved to the door, turning the light off as he came out of the room closing the door behind him. He leaned against the wall, shoving his hands down in his pockets.

The pair simply stood watching each other for several seconds. So much left unspoken, so much both were afraid to bring out into the open.

"Did Darren know about Marc?" Darius asked.

"No." She sighed and leaned back against the opposite wall. "I found out I was pregnant only shortly before he died."

"Hmmm. You couldn't have been that far along—unless…"

Liz left the question lingering in the air. She had no idea what he'd been about to say, but if it involved her relationship with Darren it couldn't be anything good.

He shook his head. "No, I would've known."

This one she couldn't resist. "Known what?"

"If you'd been sleeping with both of us at the same time, I would've known."

"Of course, I wasn't sleeping with—" Suddenly remembering where she was she lowered her voice. "Of course I wasn't sleeping with both of you at the same time!"

He shrugged. "That's what I figured."

He turned and headed toward the living room, but she grabbed his arm. "Why did you ask me that?"

"I just wondered if Darren knew. I'm sorry he didn't." He looked directly into her eyes. "A man has the right to know if he's fathered a child. Don't you think so?"

"Of course, but in this case, fate took away that right."

"What about me?"

Her eyes widened in terror, and Darius bit his lip to keep from confirming her obvious suspicion. He wasn't ready yet. He hadn't figured out how he wanted to reveal this newfound knowledge, so he continued to play dumb. "Didn't I deserve to know I had a nephew?"

"I told you—I didn't know where you were."

"Right. But you found me when you needed me, didn't you?"

"That was different. I'm pretty sure I was the last person you wanted showing up on your doorstep for a social call."

"Maybe." He closed the distance between them in two steps. Bracing his arms against the wall he trapped her in place. "Maybe not."

Darius tilted his head to the side and took in her blue-jean-clad legs. "I mean, motherhood has filled you out nicely. You use to have little skinny chicken legs—but those things, umph." He shook his head. "Those thick thighs would fit around a man's waist nice and snug."

She folded her arms across her chest but did not attempt to break out of the flesh prison.

When his eyes finally came back up to her face it was to find her studying him with curiosity. "Are you done?"

He dropped his arms and backed away. "For the moment."

"And here I was concerned because you were being such a gentleman. Should've known you couldn't keep up that charade for long."

He shoved his hands back in his pockets and looked down at the floor. "You're right. I'm sorry, I shouldn't have done that." When he looked up again, his soft brown eyes were filled with regret. "Forgive me?"

She nodded slowly.

He leaned forward and placed a gentle kiss on her forehead. "I'll see you tomorrow." He turned and headed toward the living room once again.

Liz stood in the hall and watched as he said his good-byes to Dee, and then he was gone out the door. Soon after, his rental car was pulling out of the driveway.

Liz tried to recall the look of regret in his eyes right before that apologetic kiss on the forehead. He'd said he was sorry. He'd *looked* sorry. But she knew he wasn't. He'd been lying through his pretty white teeth. She knew it as true as she knew her own name. Why? What was he up to?

She cracked the door to Marc's room to look in on him. She smiled, seeing that he'd already tossed off the covers. He was the worst sleeper she'd ever seen and usually spent most of the night traveling around to the four corners of his little bed. By morning, the covers would probably be on the floor and sometimes that's where she found her child, as well.

She shook her head and started to pull the door closed and stopped. Her eyes narrowed. *Could Darius know?*

*No,* she decided. *How could he?*

He and Darren were so similar in appearance any questions he asked could be answered by that. Feeling only slightly reassured she pulled the door closed and went to find her own bed.

# Chapter 7

"I forgot how damn cold it is here in the winter time." Darius leaned toward Liz to speak above the wind whistling around them.

"Hey, don't look for any sympathy from me. This was your idea."

"Correction—this was Marc's idea." He curled his gloved hands and blew on them. "I just wanted to build a snowman."

"Exactly. What the hell were *you* thinking?"

"I haven't built a snowman since I was a kid, I thought it would be fun. You know—like reliving a part of your childhood."

"Uh-huh. How's that working for you?"

"It was working fine until he stumbled over that dead squirrel and decided it needed a decent burial."

"It's the respectful thing to do. I'm very proud he thought of it."

The look of shock he gave her made her laugh out loud. "What? He's sensitive!"

"Too sensitive. It's a dead squirrel. I say we just dump the thing and let the vultures find it later."

"Shh. He'll hear you."

A few feet away, Marc was walking along the treeline of the backyard looking for small twigs and rocks. Dee followed a few steps behind holding the plastic bag for his collection. The pair stopped and both focused on some brown thing on the ground. A second later they were in deep discussion about it.

"Oh, God. What are they looking at now?"

Liz squinted trying to see what had captured their attention. "Don't worry, it's not another squirrel—at least, I don't think it is."

Darius sighed and looked down at the shoe box on the ground at his feet which held the partially decomposed corpse of a small, brown squirrel. "Should Marc be out here in the cold this long?"

She glanced at him, not liking the proprietary tone he'd begun taking with her son in the past couple of days. "I try to let him have as normal a life as possible. As long as he's bundled up, he'll be fine."

Darius rocked back and forth trying to warm his body. He blew on his hands again, stomped his feet and returned to the rocking, and all the while Liz watched him in fascination.

Finally she said. "You've been living on that tropical island too long. Your blood has thinned out. Why don't you just go back inside where it's warm?"

He looked at her with wide eyes. "And let him think I'm a wimp? No way."

She shook her head. "Suit yourself, but I don't think we're going anywhere until Tommy—"

"Tony. He named it Tony."

"Until Tony the squirrel gets a world-class funeral."

"Well, they better hurry up. I can't feel my toes anymore."

Liz toyed with the ends of the red knitted scarf hanging around her neck. "Can I ask you something?"

"Shoot."

"Other than the beautiful weather, why did you stay in New Zealand?"

"A lot of reasons, really." He glanced at her. "It's peaceful there. After—you know—all I wanted was a little peace and quiet, time to think." He bent and picked up a small pebble from the ground. "The first couple of days after you two left were the hardest. All the looks of sympathy, pity, everyone being nosy and gossiping—"

"Darius, I'm sorry. I didn't think about—"

"I know. Anyway, my dad kept telling me to go after you. Like, what good would that have done?"

"I kinda wish you had."

He turned to face her while toying with the pebble in his hand. Liz continued to watch her son and aunt, knowing that if she turned and looked into his eyes she might not have the courage to finish her thought.

"Things were not…when we got to Vegas—it didn't go the way I thought it would. I regretted what I'd done almost from the moment I did it. But by then it was already too late to undo it."

"I really wish you would've talked to me, Liz. I

could've told you what Darren was like. But I had no idea you two had gotten so *cozy.*"

"I was just young and stupid. It wasn't like we planned it, Darius."

He huffed loudly. "Maybe *you* didn't—but I know my brother." He tossed away the pebble.

She quickly glanced at him and looked away. "It wasn't all Darren's fault. It started as just friendship, you know. Joking around at the engagement dinner, then he suggested we have lunch together. It all started so…innocently."

"Where the hell was I during all this innocence?"

"Busy with the delis and supermarkets. It seemed like you spent ninety percent of your time doing one thing or another for one of those stores."

"I was trying to build a future for us."

"That was part of the problem, Darius. You never asked me what I wanted for the future. You just started making plans."

"Oh, so it was my fault?"

"No, that's not what I meant. Just forget it."

"No, no, this is good. I want to hear this. These questions have been driving me crazy for years. So, tell me, Liz, when did the relationship stop being innocent? *That's* the part that confuses me the most. Every time I touched you, every time we made love, you still felt like mine. Never once did I think you were with someone else."

"I told you—it wasn't like that." She took a deep breath to fortify herself and slowly turned to face him.

"Then what was it like?"

"If I told you the truth of it, you would never believe me."

"Try me."

"What's the point?" She tucked her gloved hands in her coat pocket. "Besides—"

"Mom! Uncle Darius! Look!" Marc came racing back to where they stood, with Dee walking slowly behind him. Marc opened his small hands to reveal an empty bird's nest. "We can bury Tony in this."

"Great idea, sweetheart." Liz touched his cheek. "Come on." She headed toward the other part of the large open yard. "I know just the spot."

Dee shivered and scrunched her neck down in her coat. "Think we can make this a short ceremony? It's freezing out here."

As the small group discussed several spots for the burial, Darius couldn't seem to take his eyes off Liz. He wanted to finish their discussion, but knew it was done—at least for now. What had she meant? *If I told you the truth of it, you would never believe me.* Was she about to tell him the truth about Marc?

Finally, Tony was firmly planted under a pile of twigs and rocks—seeing as the ground was too frozen to bury him beneath the earth. Darius stood listening to his son give the sweetest eulogy you could give for a dead squirrel, but at the same time his mind was spinning with contradicting thoughts.

All the strong emotions Liz had always inspired in him seemed to have returned triple-strength. Every time he saw her he wanted to take her in his arms, shake her senseless for the hurt she'd caused him and then make passionate love to her until neither of them could stand.

In one month, this woman had completely torn down all the walls he'd constructed over the past ten years to deal with the pain of losing her. And now on top of those intense emotions he was struggling to come to terms with the fact that he was a father. And that he'd been denied access or even awareness of his child for almost ten years. All those firsts he missed, all those precious moments he could never get back. Thinking about it only made him want to shake Liz senseless again, and round and round he went.

As they climbed the back-porch steps to the house, he caught Liz's arm and whispered in her ear. "We're not done."

"I know." She looked at him and the sadness in her eyes stunned him. "And knowing that terrifies me." She pulled away and went into the house.

So far, he'd spent every available moment with Marc and Liz. The idea of letting his family know he was back in the States was somewhere on the periphery of his brain. Although, after finding out how they'd treated Liz all these years, he wasn't sure he could be civil long enough for a reunion.

"Ready, champ?" He smiled at Marc, hoping his face did not reflect his concern.

The following Tuesday, Darius stood at the bedside of his son in the nursing unit of the Cleveland Clinic where the surgery was to be performed. This was the last time he would see Marc for the next couple of days while they were both recovering from the surgery.

"Yep." The boy smiled bravely, and Darius remembered the words of his mother. *He's the bravest person I know.* She was right.

He bent forward and kissed Marc's forehead, fighting back his own tears. The past two weeks they'd spent together had been perfect. They'd done the simplest things and yet he'd learned so much about his son. Like the mischievous nature and quick wit that he knew sometimes annoyed Liz. And the even quicker temper that Darius immediately recognized as his own and was shocked to see manifested in this tiny replica of himself.

His son made him think, made him reconsider things he thought he knew for certain. He couldn't help wondering *what if I'd never had a chance to know this incredible child?*

*What if...?* He shook off the morbid thoughts, just grateful to God for intervening. And at this point, he was certain it was divine intervention that had brought Liz to his island.

When she'd left Tairua to return to the States, all he'd wanted was to punish her for her betrayal. If she made him miserable on their wedding day, he would make her miserable by forcing her to go on their honeymoon. He knew it was the last thing she'd *ever* want to do. But now all he wanted was to hear her tell him that this child he already loved was his. After spending time with both of them, all he wanted was a chance to start over.

He glanced across the room to where Dee sat knitting quietly and noticed that despite her busy fingers her eyes were firmly trained on him. She smiled at him with warm, knowing eyes, and he realized that she knew he knew. Somehow...she knew he knew.

Without acknowledging the silent message, he turned to the side to quickly wipe away the tears hanging on his lashes. The last thing Marc needed going into surgery was the memory of him crying over his bed.

"Okay, that's that." Liz came walking into the room at top speed. "All the paperwork is finally done." She clapped her hands together and gave her son a bright smile. "This will be over lickity-split, and you'll be back to beating me at chess in no time."

Darius immediately recognized the nervousness she was trying to hide with her false enthusiasm and sensed that Marc did, as well. But the boy just smiled at her.

"When I'm better, Uncle Darius promised to take me to New Zealand to see dolphins."

*Damn.* The boy's timing definitely left something to be desired.

Liz suddenly swung around to face Darius with an odd expression on her pretty face. "Did he?"

Well, Darius decided, now was as good a time as any to stake his claim.

"Yes." He stepped closer to the bed. "I was thinking maybe over summer vacation you three could come visit me on the island."

Dee's eyes lit up brighter than Marc's. "Oooh, I've never been outside the United States. That sounds like a great idea."

"We'll see." Liz deliberately turned her back to him and focused on her son.

*Yes, we will.*

Marc reached up and took her hand. "Mom, I'm going to be fine. You'll see. Uncle Darius has really good kidneys. Don't you, Uncle Darius?"

"The best God makes."

"I'll be good as new, and then we can go to New Zealand because I'll be healthy again."

Darius watched Liz reach forward and cup Marc's small cheek. "Have I told you how much I love you?"

"Yes." Marc sighed dramatically. "You're not going to get all emotional, are you?" She curved her fingers under his neck and his little body twisted as laughter filled the air. "Stop! Stop, Mom! That tickles!"

"I know," Liz said, but she stopped. "Look, I'm going to go help Uncle Darius get settled in and then I'll be right back, okay?"

"Okay."

Darius waved his goodbyes to Dee, and gestured for Liz to lead the way since he had no idea where he was supposed to check in.

Marc called to Liz's retreating back. "Can I get a burger this evening?"

"No, sweetie, not tonight. But first thing—when you get out of the hospital."

He rubbed his little hands together in a sinister way, and whispered, "eexceelleennt."

"And you get in my case about Sugar Babies?" Darius whispered close to her ear.

"That's different." She frowned.

"Right." He just shook his head as she led the way out into the hall.

After they'd walked the several feet to the elevator in complete silence, Darius decided it would be up to him to break the dam. "His Mr. Burns impression is pretty good."

As he'd expected, she turned to face him, and as he'd expected, her pretty brown eyes, when filled with anger, sparkled like copper fire. He'd almost forgotten how beautiful she was in a fit. And she was definitely—in a fit.

"Why did you promise Marc he could come to New Zealand?!"

"It was just one of those things, you know. I was putting him to bed one night and he asked about where I lived."

"So you promised to *take him there?*"

"What's the big deal?"

"What's the big deal?! You can't just up and promise to take my child halfway around the world without even talking to me about it first!"

"You would've said no."

"Of course, I would've said no!" She braced her hands on her hips and leaned toward him, her eyes narrowing to slits. "I don't make him promises I can't keep. And you may not have noticed, Darius, but not everyone is doing as good as you are financially! I can't keep buying thousand-dollar airline tickets!"

*She is so hot when she's angry.* Darius struggled to keep his eyes on her face, knowing instinctively if he let them roam over her sexy body in that moment she would probably take it the wrong way. No, she would take it the *right* way, and that was the problem.

"You're overreacting."

"Am I?"

"Of course. You know I would gladly buy your tickets whenever you wanted to come. That's not the issue."

"Then what *is* the issue, Darius?!"

"You're selfish." He turned toward the elevator doors hoping to hide his increasing hard-on. Her bust was heaving with every accelerated heartbeat and it was actually requiring concentration to focus on the conversation and not just lift her against the wall and take her.

"What do you mean, I'm selfish?"

He glanced up at the elevator and realized it rested on the fifth floor and had not moved the entire time they'd been standing there. "There's something wrong with this elevator."

"What do you mean I'm selfish?"

He turned and headed toward the stairwell at the end

of the hall. "Just that. You bring me here for this surgery—which you should've done last year."

"How many times do I have to tell you I didn't know where you were!" She followed in his wake, still arguing loudly. The various staff personnel came out into the hall to see what all the commotion was, but no one interfered.

"Well, now I'm here!" He spun to face her and Liz was forced to stop suddenly to avoid colliding with him. "What did you think? I was just going to slink back off into the night when it's over?"

The reminder that that was *exactly* what she'd intended managed to cool his lust slightly. She had no intention of him ever knowing Marc was his. And she had no intention of him being a part of the boy's life— not even as an uncle.

They reached the stairwell entrance and Darius swung the door open to enter.

"Where are you going?!"

"Hell if I know!" He called back and started down the stairs, his anger building with every step. If she thought she could keep him out of his son's life, she had another thought coming.

Hands braced on hips she glared down at him. "Pre-op is upstairs, you idiot."

He stopped. Took several deep breaths to calm himself. Then turned and slowly walked back up the flight of stairs until they were standing almost nose to nose.

"Do not push me, Liz. Don't—push—me."

She chuckled and her eyes widened in amazement. "Is that a threat?"

"You will *not* keep him from me," he hissed between his teeth. "I won't allow it."

Something in her eyes registered recognition. She opened her mouth to speak and then quickly closed it. The pair stood so close their breath mingled in the cool air of the stairwell. Neither backing down, neither seemed willing to give an inch.

Finally Darius turned and headed up the stairs taking them two at a time, the pain in his back jaw signaling that he was gritting his teeth. He didn't hear Liz's footsteps behind him, but assumed she was still following.

Darius was determined to control his anger. This was neither the time nor the place for a confrontation. He still had no idea what the proper way was to handle the Marc thing, but blurting the truth in a hospital stairwell was not it.

He reached the next landing and waited before entering the floor. Slowly, she came up the stairs. Her forehead wrinkled with a frown, but she said nothing.

"Is this the floor?" he asked.

She nodded up to indicate that they still had one more flight to take. He turned to go up and she stopped him with her words.

"He's all I have."

Darius paused on the stairs, and silence settled around them once more. Slowly he turned to face her, hoping the compassion he felt was reflected on his face. "I know that. I'm not trying to take him, I just want to be a part of his life."

She walked past him and sat down on the step. Darius just stood watching her knowing something important was about to be said.

She looked up at him with tears in her eyes. "How did you know?"

# Chapter 8

Okay, Darius thought, so apparently a hospital stairwell *would* be the place for this confrontation. He walked over and leaned against the wall next to her. "His birthmark."

"What birthmark?"

"On his lower back. I saw it one night when he was crawling into bed."

She frowned in confusion as if still not understanding.

"No one in my family has that mark but me—not even Darren had it."

"A mark? That doesn't prove anything."

He folded his arms across his chest. "Maybe not, but the guilt in your eyes right now sure does."

"A birthmark." She shook her head as if unable to believe she'd been outdone by something so small. "I could tell you knew. The way you've been with him lately—I could tell, but I didn't want to believe it."

"Why didn't you tell me he was mine when you came to Tairua?"

"You wouldn't have believed me. You would've thought I was just saying it to get something from you and then you would've demanded a paternity test. I wasn't about to put Marc through all that. I was hoping that any similarities you saw, you would assume were because you and Darren were brothers."

"Do you hear what you're saying? You weren't concerned about Marc being put through anything, Liz. Not this time. This time it was all about you. You would deny me my son, and Marc his father because it might make your life a little uncomfortable."

"That's not true."

"Isn't it?"

"No!"

"Think about it. Even if I did ask for a paternity test—that's just a little blood. He would've never even known what it was for. No, you were worried about what would come after the test confirmed the truth. You were worried that you would have to share Marc."

"You're so different now." She shook her head sadly. "When I came to Tairua I was planning to tell you, but then I saw you talking to some guest and you seemed so...cold."

He huffed. "Thanks to you and Marc, I'm thawing—fast."

"I'm serious, Darius. With your money we both know if you wanted, you could—"

"Wait a minute." He knelt before her. "That's not going to happen. I would never try to take him away from you. But I do want to be a part of his life. And...I want to be a part of your life."

The silence was palpable. Her eyes widened in horror, and Darius felt like a balloon that had suddenly been stabbed with a pin. All the soft warmth radiating in his heart suddenly disappeared. He stood up and looked down at her.

"Okay, I get it. I may not be the man you want. But that doesn't change the fact that I am the man who fathered your child. I *will* be a part of Marc's life, Liz, so you might as well wrap your head around the idea." He gestured up the steps. "Let's get going, they're waiting for me in pre-op."

He moved around her and headed up the stairs. Well, he thought, at least now he knew which way the wind blew. For a while there he was starting to believe she still wanted him as much as he wanted her, but that dream had just died a quick death.

Even after all these years and everything they'd revealed to each other it still came down to the original problem. In the end, he was not the man she'd chosen, the man she wanted. He was not Darren.

Despite his brother's obvious infidelity—because Darren didn't know how to be faithful—and who knows whatever else went on in Vegas, despite all that, she still loved the bastard.

He reached the landing and opened the door leading into the hospital. Fine, if that was how she felt there was nothing he could do about it. Because no woman on earth was worth the humiliation of competing against his dead brother's ghost.

Liz leaned against the windowsill of the hospital waiting room, listening as the sloshing combination of snow and ice pelted the glass. The two men in her life were only forty-five minutes into the three-hour surgery and her emotions were already a tangled mess.

Dee sat on the other side of the room knitting away as if she didn't have a care in the world, but Liz could see the slight tremble as her deft fingers worked. She had no comfort to offer her aunt. She needed every little bit for herself.

The agonizing long minutes left her with nothing better to do than to repeatedly play out the earlier conversation with Darius in her head. Could it have gone any differently? Were there words she should've used instead? Why was it that when it came to Darius her thought processes seem to malfunction and she always, always made the wrong choices. Always.

When she'd left for Tairua she knew there was a likelihood that Darius would want to be a part of Marc's life after the surgery. She had, to some degree, mentally prepared herself for that reality. She understood that by asking for his help she might be bringing him back into their lives permanently.

At the time it had seemed a small surrender. But to know something with your mind and to feel it with your heart were two entirely different experiences. After the past two weeks she now understood that what Darius wanted was not small at all.

Somehow, in all her planning and preparation she had not anticipated the emotional effect of coming face-to-face with him again. Nor had she accounted for all the ways life might have changed him over the years. Or how those two factors would affect *her* life.

She'd had no inkling of the tidal wave of regret and resentment simmering just beneath the surface of her controlled exterior even after all these years. Or, that he would *still* look at her with eyes filled with the pain of her betrayal.

It was as if the past ten years had never happened and they were stuck in some kind of time loop together. For all her thoughtful planning, there was so much she could've never planned for. Things that in hindsight seemed obvious.

Like the fact that a boy who'd primarily been raised by a single mom and a great-aunt, would, of course, latch on to the first male relative he'd ever known with an almost superhero-type worship.

She could not have predicted that the love she had for Darius, the love she'd thought she'd buried years ago would resurface in her heart like a dormant volcano springing to life once again. And along with that intense love, the heartbreak of knowing he still despised her. Still.

She glanced out the window at the busy city below, wondering at the significance of his promise to Marc. Try as she might, she could not reconcile the Darius she'd seen that first day on the island with the man who tucked her son in at night. She wasn't sure which was the real Darius. Having developed a suspicious nature over the years, Liz leaned toward believing he was really the man from Tairua. And if she was right…then she was headed for a world of pain.

He wanted revenge for what she'd done, and justifiable as his anger may've been, it hurt to know nonetheless. So how could she believe him? How could she ever trust him? *I want to be a part of your life.* How could she accept that when she already knew how far he was willing to go to get his revenge? Seven days in paradise.

No, for Marc's sake and her own, she could not allow herself to become vulnerable to whatever he had planned. But how could she not be? How was she supposed to keep her part of the bargain and her heart at the same time?

Darius awoke from the surgery to find himself apparently alone in the recovery room, not that it surprised him. He wasn't exactly expecting Liz to be sitting by his bedside hanging on his every breath with her son in surgery, as well. And after the tense moments in the stairwell earlier, he wondered if he'd ruined any chance he may have had with her. Or, if he'd ever had a chance at all.

He glanced down at the IV inserted in his arm, and the patch attached to his chest that had cords hooked to a large machine beside the bed. The pain in his stomach was intense, but tolerable and he assumed he must've been given some pretty strong painkillers.

"How are you feeling?" A voice from the corner of the room startled him. Darius turned his head to find Dee sitting quietly a few feet away, knitting as usual.

He struggled to sit up in the bed to better see her. "Not bad." He glanced at the clock and was surprised to find it almost eight in the evening. "How long have you been here?"

"A few hours." She stood, putting her knitting to the side, and came to stand at the bedside. "The doctors said the surgery went really well." She smiled. "Marc's body accepted the kidney without trouble so—" A small frown creased her brow before she quickly hid the expression.

It was no use denying it, Darius knew what she was thinking, what she'd almost said. *So far.* Marc's young body was accepting the kidney for now, but they all knew it would be weeks before he was completely out of danger.

"That's wonderful." He struggled to shift, but the pain stopped him immediately.

Dee reached forward to help. "You should lie still, your body's been through a lot. Can I get something for you? Some water?"

"Water sounds good." He slumped back down in the bed.

Dee walked to a nearby table and poured some water from a pitcher into a small plastic cup. "Should I call the nurse?"

"No, I'm fine. Thanks." Darius accepted the water and gulped it down quickly.

She reached forward and touched his cheek. "You did a good thing today, Darius."

"I just wish Liz would've come to me sooner."

"She was scared I think." Dee shook her head in confusion. "Scared of facing you. Scared of losing Marc. Eventually one fear overcame the other. In the beginning, when Marc was first put on the transplant list I don't think she realized how difficult it would be to find a match for him, or how long it would take."

Darius glanced at the older woman, noting her faraway expression. She was reliving moments in her minds, probably the past few years of watching her greatnephew suffer. Darius decided to take advantage of her talkative mood. "How is Liz affording his care? She can't make that much as a teacher, even with those benefits."

"You've seen how we live."

"Still…" His eyes narrowed in concentration. "Living sparsely doesn't seem like it would be enough. Is she getting any help from anyone?"

Dee smiled. "Darius, are you trying to find out if Liz has a sugar daddy?"

"Not really, I was thinking her parents." He frowned. "But now that you mention it, does she?"

Dee's soft brown eyes turned cold. "No, no help from that worthless pair. They wouldn't lift a finger to help her. More concerned about their precious image than their own child." She pulled a chair closer to the bed and took a seat. "When Darren died Liz came back to Cincinnati, not because she wanted to, but because of Marc. Her own parents wouldn't even let her spend a night under their roof. Can you believe that? Their only daughter—and grandchild." She huffed. "Said she had disgraced them. Said they didn't have a daughter anymore." She folded her arms across her chest. "That's how she ended up at my place. All I had was a small apartment, but it was big enough for the three of us."

Darius frowned realizing how little he knew about Liz's aunt. Only that she was her father's sister and a bit of a recluse. "Do you have any children, Dee?"

She shook her head. "No, never could get pregnant. After my second husband, I just stopped trying." She looked directly into his eyes. "That's why I will never understand my fool brother and his wife turning their backs on Liz."

Darius frowned. "I don't understand either. Did she go to my parents for help? Did she tell them about Marc? They never said anything about him when I talked to them. All I know is what they told me when they called."

"Oh, she went to them all right. And they did the same thing her own parents did. They turned their backs on her and their grandchild. As far as the Donovans and Norths were concerned, Darren and Liz no longer existed." She quickly glanced at him and looked away. "You made it even easier."

"What do you mean?"

"Well, with you moving away so quickly, they were able to put the whole ugly incident behind them and pretend it never happened. Soon, their country-club friends stopped talking about it and their sorry little lives returned to normal." She snorted. "If you call that normal."

Darius's eyes narrowed as his mind worked through what it must've been like for Liz returning home to find she had no home to return to. He reached over the side of the bed and took Dee's hand in his. "Thank you."

"No, thank *you.*" Her eyes narrowed on his face. "I know you know the truth about Marc. So what are you going to do about it?"

Darius decided there was no point in lying about it. He'd seen the truth in her eyes before the surgery. "I'm going to be a father to my son."

Dee shook her head. "It won't be that easy."

"What do you mean?"

"Liz is nervous about your intentions, and she's very protective of Marc."

"I know that."

"No, I don't think you do. She's changed, Darius. Life had hardened her and that boy is the center of her world. If she feels you are a threat to that world…" She shook her head sadly.

Darius tilted his head considering her words. It felt like a warning. "Go on."

"Like I said—she's changed."

Darius looked at the older woman wondering what subtle message she was trying to send. Was she warning him away? Or telling him to tread lightly? Either way, he needed her to understand he would not under any circumstances be kept away from his son.

"I've changed as well, Dee."

She nodded. "I know. I see it in you. You're more human now."

He frowned. "What the hell is that suppose to mean?"

"I didn't see you that often, but I remember what you were like. So caught up in your plans and ambitions, you didn't notice much else."

That message hit the mark. "You're the second person to accuse me of that. What happened between Liz and Darren was *not* because I was not paying attention."

"I never said it was. It's just that from my point of view it seemed like Liz was more of a prop in your life, not really anything important to you, just something you needed to move your plans forward."

"That is not true!" He struggled to sit up again, but the pain shooting through his body became unbearable. "I love Liz!" For some reason the accusation stung like a burn in his chest.

"Slow down." Dee stood and gently placed her hand on his chest. "You're gonna hurt yourself."

"Liz was not a prop for me! She was the most important thing in my life!"

"Did you ever tell her that?"

"Yes! With a ring!"

A nurse appeared in the doorway. "Everything okay in here?" She crossed to the bed, her sharp eyes taking in the recordings of the machines. "Mr. North, you're going to have to calm down now." She glanced at Dee. "What's going on here?"

Dee's faced twisted with regret. "I'm sorry, I didn't mean to upset him."

"I'm going to have to ask you to leave," the nurse said sternly, but Darius put his hand up.

"Wait! Don't send her away." He sighed. "I'll relax." He took a deep breath. "See? Better already."

"You really need to rest, Mr. North." The nurse's lip firmed in a thin line of determination.

"I know, I will. I just need to talk to her privately for a minute."

The nurse glanced between the pair as though considering what to do.

"Please, just a few moments more," he pleaded.

"Fine." The nurse turned to Dee. "And then, you need to leave and let him rest."

"I will," Dee reassured the nurse's retreating back as she left the room. She turned back to Darius. "I'm sorry, I really didn't mean to upset you."

Darius's mind had turned inward, but he still heard her. "It's okay, Dee, I think I needed upsetting."

# Chapter 9

Later that day, Darius was beginning to feel the effects of some recently administered painkillers when he felt a presence in the room. He opened his eyes to find Liz standing beside the bed watching him with watery eyes.

"How's Marc?" His drowsy voice startled her.

"I thought you were asleep." Liz smiled, and the water spilled over to her cheek. "He's doing fine."

"Good."

"How are you?"

"Good. The doctor said I should be released in three days."

"That's standard. Marc should be coming home around the same time." She toyed with the arm of the bed. "Darius, I want you to come home with us when you leave here."

"No, Liz, thanks, but I couldn't impose on you that

way. And in a few days I'll be heading back to New Zealand anyway."

Her eyebrows crinkled in confusion. "Already?"

"I've been away too long as it is."

She shook her head firmly. "Okay—but I insist you stay with us until you leave."

"Liz, really—"

"I insist."

"All right. If you insist." Darius sighed, knowing he was in no shape to argue with her, and besides, the idea of spending his recovery time alone in a sterile hotel room, as opposed to spending it in Liz's cozy, small home with his son didn't come close to being appealing.

"Look…about what happened earlier in the stairwell."

"Forget it." Darius turned his head away and reached for his water cup. The sting of that particular burn was still too fresh, and he had no intention of letting her know that she could still inflict that kind of hurt on him. "We were both angry and it got out of hand. But I meant what I said, Liz, I want to be a part of Marc's life." He glanced at her. "It bothers me that he calls me Uncle Darius. What is he going to think when he learns the truth?"

"You think I don't worry about that?"

"We need to explain it to him in a way he can understand."

"I'll explain it to him."

"When?"

"Soon."

"Three months."

"What?"

"In three months you'll be coming to Tairua, and if you haven't told him the truth by then, I will."

They simply stared at each other, the silent challenge was palpable.

His eyes narrowed. "I mean it. You have three months to tell him the truth, Liz. One way or another my son *will* grow up knowing who his father is. Are we clear?"

"Perfectly," she said softly, then turned and started toward the door. "I just wanted to check and see how you were doing. Just let the nurse know if you need anything and I'll see you at check out."

"Liz."

She paused in the doorway.

"If you want to withdraw the invitation to stay at your house, I'll understand."

"Why would I do that?"

He simply looked at her knowing they both knew why.

"One thing has nothing to do with the other, Darius. You have given my son something no one else could, and for that I will always be grateful. The fact that you require a price for it shouldn't surprise me. After all, making a profit has *always* been your highest priority."

A week later, Darius lay on one end of the couch in Liz's small living room examining the chess board on the small fold-away tray between him and the other convalescent resting on a loveseat across from him.

"Uncle Darius, do you plan to move anytime today?"

"Don't rush me, boy," Darius grumbled, still examining the board.

"You take longer than Mom."

A snicker came from the other end of the couch where Liz was sitting with her legs folded beneath her, grading test papers.

"Considering your last two games with him, I wouldn't snicker too loudly," Darius said.

This time a snicker came from across the room, where Dee sat knitting what would eventually be a man's sweater.

Darius chose his move and as soon as he lifted his hand, Marc took his move and called checkmate.

Darius looked at Liz in stunned amazement. "Did you see that?"

"I didn't have to. He's tricked me like that too many times to count."

Marc laughed loudly. "I win! Again! You lose—I win! I'm a winner, and you're—"

Darius pointed a stern finger at his son. "*Don't* say it."

Marc's only response was more laughter.

Darius stretched and a loud yawn slipped out. He immediately regretted it as everyone took it as a signal to clear out.

Liz stood from her position on the end of the couch and Darius could not resist letting his eyes roam over her shapely blue-jean-clad bottom. It was too easy to remember all the many nights he'd held those firm cheeks in the palms of his hands. So long ago, and yet it felt like yesterday.

Dee began gathering up her supplies and packing them away, as well.

"Really, you all don't have to leave. I'm not sleepy. It was just a little yawn."

"You need your rest," Liz said, picking up the pile of bedding neatly folded beside the couch.

"Do I have to go to bed?" Marc whined. "I don't have any school tomorrow. Can't I stay up?"

"Absolutely not, young man. You may be off this

week but we're staying on your schedule. Monday will be here before you know it. Now, go brush your teeth."

"Night, Uncle Darius." Marc turned with slumped shoulders and wandered toward the bathroom.

"Liz, really. You don't have to shut down the whole household every time I rub my eyes."

"You need to rest, Darius," Dee called back over her shoulder heading to her basement apartment. "You've got a ways to go before you'll be back to full strength."

Darius looked up at Liz realizing they were alone for the first time since Marc and he had come home from the hospital. She stood with her hands on her slender hips and he knew that he had no chance of winning this argument.

He stood and began making the couch into a bed as he did every night.

"Sure you don't want any help?" Liz offered as she did every night.

"No, thanks. You've done enough."

"Okay." She turned and headed down the hallway toward her bedroom. "See you in the morning."

"Liz?"

She turned at the sound of her name.

"After Darren, why didn't you ever marry? I mean you're only thirty." He tossed the sheet over the couch and began tucking it in.

Her eyes widened slightly in surprise. "I don't feel thirty." She laughed, and shrugged her shoulders. "Beside, I guess I never really considered it. With work and Marc and school, where was I suppose to find time to date?"

He tossed the pillows to the head of the couch, and stood staring at her for several long seconds. "I just wondered."

"What about you?" She leaned against the wall, folding her arms across her chest. "Why didn't you ever marry?"

He picked up the blanket as his mind wandered back. He smirked. "I came close once."

"Really?"

"Yeah, she was a local real estate agent. Smart, beautiful and we seemed to be a good fit." He sat down on the sheet, still holding the blanket in his arms.

"What happened?"

"Turns out she had a little nervous condition."

"What kind of nervous condition?"

"When she got stressed out at work, or if we'd have an argument, a day or so later my guests would complain about their possessions coming up missing."

Liz covered her mouth in shock.

"Being the fiancée of the hotel owner, she had complete access to my master keys. I mean, I never hid them from her, didn't realize there was any need to."

"What happened?"

"When I realized it was her, I confronted her and she totally broke down. She broke off the engagement, said she'd been doing this type of thing for years, and now she just wanted to concentrate on getting help."

Liz crossed the room and sat down beside him. "Oh, Darius, I'm so sorry."

"Hey." He shrugged. "Life happens."

"We're quite a pair, huh?" Liz chuckled.

"Yes, we are." He smiled, looking at her pretty face. Darius felt an almost overwhelming desire to lean forward and kiss her, but remembering the stairwell incident he fought it down. "Do you miss Darren?"

Liz reached up and ran her hands through her long hair, shaking it free of the small scrunchy that was barely holding it back. "No, not really. I hope that doesn't sound terrible. But, I realized…afterward, that I didn't really know him at all." She leaned her head against his shoulder, and Darius sat perfectly still, not wanting to give her a single reason to move. "He died before either of us could change that. It's hard to miss someone you never really knew.

"Do you miss your fiancée?" she asked on a yawn.

"I don't know if *miss* is the right word. I wish I had done more to help her."

As if suddenly realizing what she was doing—leaning on his shoulder and fast on her way to sleep—Liz bolted to an upright position. "Well, I'm heading to bed. See you in the morning."

"Okay." He returned to making up the couch.

Liz headed down the hall to her bedroom, thinking over what she'd just been told. In all their conversations, somehow it had not occurred to her that Darius might've been engaged to someone else. She wasn't sure why she'd never considered it, after all, it made complete sense. He was gorgeous, successful and generous. Hell, if she hadn't been such a fool she would've gone ahead with their wedding all those years ago.

But somehow, knowing he'd had another failed relationship only made her feel worse, as if she were somehow to blame. She peeked into Marc's room and found him leaning over a toybox. "Get to bed, sweetheart."

He didn't move, and her heart skipped a beat as she hurried across the room to him. She stopped suddenly and took a deep breath at the sound of the soft snoring coming from the toybox. With a shake of her head, Liz gathered her sleeping son in her arms and carried him to his bed.

Tucking his covers around his small body, she smiled as she noticed the bruised areas on his arms were beginning to fade. Gently, she leaned forward and kissed the small spots that were still slightly bruised, and said a silent prayer that the days of dialysis were now behind them.

Standing, she kissed his forehead and headed across the hall to her own room. She paused and glanced back toward the living room, which was now dark. Apparently, both her patients were more tired than they thought.

Liz lay in bed staring at the ceiling for almost two hours before she finally realized she would not be falling asleep anytime soon. There was too much running through her head and she replayed the last few weeks over and over in her mind. And not only the last few weeks; she found her thoughts wandering back further and further.

She remembered the anger and disdain on the faces of her parents when she'd come home from Vegas, and her amazement when they'd slammed the door in the faces of her and her infant son without the slightest hesitation, without the slightest regret that they were abandoning not only her, but their grandchild. Of everything that had happened to her over the past years, the rejection by her parents was perhaps the most shocking. She'd just always assumed they would forgive her anything. But apparently, public humiliation was the deal-breaker.

She thought back to when Marc was just a toddler, and the cramped one-bedroom apartment she'd shared with Dee. What would she have done if Dee had not opened her home and heart to them? She remembered the fear and excitement she'd experienced as she'd filled out the registration for school that first time. She re-

membered the mild reaction she'd had to the news that
Marc was diabetic. Back then, she'd had no real understanding of the disease or what it could do to a body.
But by the time he'd been diagnosed with kidney failure
she understood, and terror had gripped her heart.

Her life had changed so much over the past ten years
and yet, in some ways, not at all. Certainly, having
Darius here with her only served to remind her of the
past. But that wasn't a bad thing, she was finding. The
qualities in him she'd found boring as a teenage girl
were now comforting and reassuring to the grown
woman she'd become. Darius was the kind of man you
could depend on, she'd always known that. But now she
appreciated the value of that quality in a man. He
wanted to be a father to Marc, and having toed the line
alone for so long, it was nice to have someone willing
and able to help.

She folded her arms behind her head, lying there in the
dark remembering just how long it had been since she'd
been with a man. She tried calculating by months, thinking
somehow it sounded better if broken down into months.
She sighed. Nope, pathetic anyway you counted it.

Why? Despite what she'd told Darius, in nine years
there had certainly been opportunities for something, if
no more than the occasional fling. So, why had she
rebuked every advance, every come-on in the past one
hundred and eight months?

For the same reason she'd not been able to bring
herself to being with Darren. Every woman had at least
one secret she would take to the grave with her and for
Liz, she knew her true relationship with Darren would
be the one. While everyone she knew, including Darius,
assumed there had been a torrid affair between them,

ending in them running off to be together, only two people knew that they'd never once had sex, and of the two people, one was dead. And after all, who would ever believe it?

Looking back, Liz now understood that the desire to bed her was Darren's only reason for taking her with him to Las Vegas. To him she was a challenge, a conquest. And keeping her in Vegas was the prize. There was never anything deeper going on with him. Looking back, Liz now understood that for her Darren had been an escape hatch, nothing more. They'd not only lied and deceived everyone they loved, they'd lied and deceived each other and themselves, as well.

*What a mess,* she thought. For the most part, Liz had accepted the poor choices of her past long ago and moved on, but with Darius here she was finding herself reliving it all over and over. And on nights like tonight, the memories were too vivid to allow rest.

Finally, she climbed out of bed, heading to the kitchen to get a glass of water, when sounds from the living room caught her attention. Going to the end of the hallway, she saw the flickering lights of the television and realized Darius was sitting up against the arm of the couch watching it.

"What're you watching?" she asked, coming into the room.

Darius quickly picked up the remote and turned down the volume. "Sorry, did I wake you?"

"No, I couldn't sleep either." She stopped at the end of the couch, staring down at the top of his head. "So, what are you watching?"

*"Cops."*

He glanced up at her. "Watching the people on it

makes me feel better about myself." He moved his legs to make room on the couch. "Care to join me, my fellow insomniac?"

She laughed. "Why not?" Sitting down beside him, she unconsciously scooted to the far corner. She could see Darius noticed, but he said nothing.

"So, why can't you sleep?" he asked, focusing his attention on the high-speed chase playing out on the screen.

She shrugged. "I don't know, just too wired, I guess. What about you?"

A small smile came to his mouth. "Sure you want to know?"

Liz felt a small stirring of excitement and considered giving a safe answer of no, but she'd been safe for so long. "Yes."

"I remember you." He glanced at her and then back at the TV. "I remember how we would curl up together on the couch in my apartment on nights like tonight watching movies and holding each other. And I remember how we'd end the evening. So much has changed, Liz, and in some ways nothing has changed."

"I know what you mean. I feel the same way. But the things that have changed are too big for us."

"What do you mean?"

"Be honest, Darius…do you think you could ever trust me again?"

Darius kept his attention focused on the television.

She sighed in disappointment. "That's why I pulled away from you in the stairwell. Not because I'm not still attracted to you, but because I remember that look in your eyes when you first realized it was me you were seeing on the beach in New Zealand. I remember the anger and resentment you felt at that moment."

"A lot has happened since then."

"Not enough."

"In what way?"

"You haven't forgiven me."

He gestured to the surrounding room. "How can you say that after the past few weeks?"

"The past few weeks have been great. You are wonderful with Marc, and I will never be able to thank you enough for what you've done." She touched his shoulder and he turned to look at her. "But in three months, you're still going to expect me to show up in New Zealand and keep my end of the bargain. Not because you really expect payment for what you did, but because you want me to pay for what I did. Does that sound like a man who has forgiven?"

His lips firmed to a thin line. "I understand what you're saying, but I'm not letting you out of it."

"See what I mean?"

"You have it all wrong. I know how it sounds, but it's not like that."

"Really? Then what is it like, Darius?"

"I don't know, but it's not about revenge. Okay, it was in the beginning, but not now."

She chuckled. "You keep telling yourself that. It's okay. I'll come to New Zealand, and keep my part of the deal, but you don't trust me. And quite frankly," she huffed, "if I were in your shoes I probably wouldn't trust me either."

"So, what are you saying?"

She leaned forward and gently touched her lips to his before pulling back. "I'm saying that because of everything that has come before, seven days in paradise is all we will ever have."

"I don't agree."

"No offense, Darius." She stood from the couch. "But you don't have to."

# Chapter 10

A week later, Liz, Dee and Marc returned from a shopping trip to find a note and an envelope attached to the front door. Liz handed Dee the envelope and opened the note.

It was from Darius, explaining that something to do with the hotel had caused him to rush home, and that he was sorry he had not had time to say goodbye.

As she read the note aloud, Liz almost hated Darius for the hurt expression she saw appearing on her son's face. Until she reached the bottom of the letter and read the final sentence to herself. Before she could decide what to do about it, Dee was laughing happily.

"Look!" She'd opened the envelope and found what the note described. Three round-trip tickets to New Zealand, dated ahead almost three months exactly to the day. Dee and Marc were bouncing around in excitement, her fifty-year-old aunt as exuberant as a child at the thought of this trip of a lifetime.

"I don't have a passport!" Dee suddenly realized. She turned to Liz. "Do you think I can get one in time?"

Liz decided to grab on to the opportunity to get out of taking her family with her. She shook her head sadly. "I don't think so. And Marc doesn't have one either."

Dee's eyebrows crinkled in confusion and disappointment, and Liz suddenly felt the size of an ant. Dee saw right through her. Liz forced a smile. "But we'll try."

With that mild assurance, Marc's spirits lifted once again, but Dee continued to watch her with suspicion as they all entered the house. Liz's mind was working overtime trying to figure out Darius's angle. Why was he inviting Dee and Marc to witness her humiliation? Unless he really did not have humiliation in mind? Either he'd meant what he said that night they'd talked, or he was a harder, colder man than she'd ever imagined. Unfortunately, Liz realized, it would be three months before she would know which answer was right.

Later than evening Darius's rented car pulled into Cincinnati and he was surprised to find how the city had changed in his absence. It took him a little longer than he expected to find his way home because many of the familiar landmarks of his childhood had been renovated into something else or wiped away completely.

As he pulled into the driveway of his parents' Colonial home, he was surprised to see several other cars parked there. He considered waiting until morning to come back, but decided he wanted this awkward confrontation over as soon as possible.

He sat in the car for a long time, simply staring at the

door. He'd been working on what he wanted to say to his parents ever since Liz had returned to his life. But now that he was here, he found that it wasn't so easy. After all, this was the home of his childhood. This was where he'd grown up in the loving protective bosom of his family. This is where he and Darren had once been friends. But for all those memories, now it felt as if he were visiting strangers.

Finally, he got out of the car and climbed the few stairs to the front door. Once again he paused. For a moment, he considered leaving without them ever knowing he'd been there. Maybe he should just leave the past in the past, and leave them always wondering why he'd never returned. But he couldn't do that. He needed to be here, for himself and for Liz. There were things that needed to be said and questions that needed to be answered.

He knocked on the door and waited patiently. When his mother answered her face spread into the familiar smile of his childhood, and Darius realized he'd been waiting for this moment for years, seeing his mother again. But now, knowing how she'd treated Liz and his son, somehow it just wasn't as pleasant an experience as he'd expected.

"Hi, Mom."

"Darius? Darius!" She rushed forward and wrapped him in a tight hug. "What are you doing here? Why didn't you tell us you were coming?"

"It was an unexpected trip." He returned the hug. "Sorry, I didn't know you were having guests over, or I would've called first."

"Don't be ridiculous." She pulled him into the house, closing the door behind him. Darius could hear voices and laughter coming from the main dining room. "It's just the Winters and the Don—" She quickly glanced at her son and looked away. "The Winters and the Donovans."

"Really." Darius's eyes narrowed on the hall leading to the main dining room. "That's good, I wanted to talk to Will Donovan, as well."

"Oh?" Carol North looked up at her only living son with a strange expression. "What did you have to talk to Will about?"

"Excuse me, Mom." He moved past her and walked deliberately down the hall, feeling his resolve strengthening with every step. "Hello, everyone," he said to the small group sitting around the dining-room table, playing cards.

"Darius! When did you get to town?" Jim North stood from the table and came to approach his son, but Darius held up his hand.

Jim stopped short. "What's wrong, son?"

"I just came from Columbus."

Will looked to someone behind Darius, and he realized his mother had followed him back into the room.

His fist formed a ball as he watched Will and Marian Donovan exchange annoyed glances. The callousness with which they'd treated their own daughter was dumbfounding. Even with what he'd been told by Liz and Dee, never did he imagine it could be true. Somewhere in the back of his mind, he'd thought that maybe her parents just hadn't realized how dire her circumstances had been. Now, he understood, if Liz had died with Darren that day they couldn't have cared any less.

The only people who didn't seem to understand the importance of the Columbus reference were Rob and Ann Winters, who only looked at the others in confusion.

Will Donovan stood from the table and folded his arms across his chest. "Look, son, if you're here to scold us, you can save your breath. Elizabeth is my child, and I will deal with her the way I see fit."

Darius took two steps forward. "No, Will, I'm not here to scold you, I'm here to put you on notice. All of you."

His father frowned. "What's that supposed to mean?"

"My son came this close to dying." He held his thumb and index finger a centimeter apart. "This close! And not one of you would've lifted a finger to help him."

"Your son?" Carol whispered from behind him.

"Yes, Mom." He turned to his mother. "Liz's child, Marc, is my son—not Darren's, as you all assumed."

"But, I thought—"

Darius cut his mother off. "I know what you thought. What you all thought. But never once did you bother to find out the truth, not that it would've made any difference to any of you. I just thought you should know." He turned back to the group. "I thought you should all know."

Darius simply shook his head at the callousness. "Do you have any idea how sick your grandchild was?" He turned in a circle, watching each face for some sign of compassion. "Do any of you care?"

"I lost my daughter when she ran off with your brother!" Marian said firmly.

"Then it's your loss, Marian. Because my son is an amazing kid, and you're going to miss out on his whole life, and that of your only child." He shook his head and looked at his father. "Darren was the only one to die, but thanks to your cold hearts you managed to lose two sons."

"What did she say to you to turn you against us?" Carol moved closer to him to put her arms around him, but Darius pulled away.

"Not much, she just told me the truth, and your behavior told me the rest." He lifted his hands in defeat. "I've said what I came here to say. I know what you did, and you won't get away with it."

"What the hell are you talking about?" Jim snapped, folding his arms across his broad chest. Darius realized that this man was the model he'd chosen for so many years, and in some ways he'd turned out just like his father. But not in the most important one, because there was no way he would ever turn his back on his child. Never.

"You turned your back on the two people I love most in this world. You left them to fend for themselves and if it hadn't been for Liz's resourcefulness, who knows where they would've ended up? I won't forget that."

"How can you stand here and defend her after what she did to you?" Carol asked, still reaching for her son.

"You'd never understand, Mom. I realize that now. None of you will ever be able to see what you did wrong because you view the world through the narrow prism of your own self-interest.

"But it's okay, they have me now, and I will never let them down the way you did." He turned to leave and paused. Turning back to the group, he said, "You know, Liz keeps saying I have a hard time forgiving people who cross me." He frowned thoughtfully. "She may be right."

"Darius! Don't leave like this!" Carol called behind him. "Son! Stay and let's talk our way through this."

Darius simply kept walking, knowing the time for talking was over. He was right, he knew it just by looking into their eyes. They would never understand why their actions were wrong. They all felt completely justified given the embarrassment Liz and Darren had brought on their families. It was all about them, always had been, their lifestyle, their children, all props to make them look better until the prop stopped working, and then it was easily and quickly tossed aside.

Later that evening, as he settled back in his seat for the long flight home, Darius realized how close he'd come to turning out just like them. As much as he hated to admit it, ten years ago, his delis and supermarkets had been his main concern. Liz had been a prop. He'd loved her, true enough. But he'd asked her to marry him because he thought she would be the perfect wife to suit his planned lifestyle. And just like his parents and hers, when she did not fall in line, instead of trying to find out what went wrong, he'd simply tossed her away and gone on with his life.

Well, he thought, she wasn't on her own anymore.

Driving down the avenue, Liz's mind was racing and she was growing more nervous by the day. There was only one more week before they were scheduled to leave for New Zealand. Much to her dismay, she'd been able to get Marc and Dee passports with relative ease. And the major airline strike she'd been praying for hadn't panned out either. She'd put in for vacation from her current job, teaching a fifth-grade English summer class, hoping her boss would reject the request but he'd just smiled, made some comment about how much she needed a break and signed off on it with no problem. Unfortunately, everything was moving along smoothly.

She pulled into the parking lot of her dry cleaners and turned off the car. She'd bought a few new outfits for the trip, but was still mostly depending on her elementary-teacher's wardrobe, which meant picking up a few things from the cleaners.

Even after weeks of contemplation, she had no idea what to expect when they arrived in New Zealand. What did seven days in paradise with Darius mean? She frowned thoughtfully. "A week in a tropical paradise… with Darius?"

Liz tilted her head to the side, realizing for the first time that somehow the full implication of this little wager had not hit her. Up until now, she'd only considered this from *his* vantage point, never thinking of what *she* stood to gain from it. After ten long, bone-dry years…could it be…was the drought about to be over?

She closed her eyes remembering what it was like to make love to Darius. Even after all these years the experience was still fresh to her senses—the feel of him, the scent and taste of him, maybe because those smells and feelings had so recently been within her reach. But, for whatever reason, she now understood that this was not only Darius's chance for satisfaction—it was hers as well. If she played her hand right.

Despite what he'd said before he left, Liz felt she understood what was in his heart. He wanted payback, and not even the discovery of his son had changed that. If she were totally honest with herself she knew that if humiliation and degradation were truly what he'd planned, he wouldn't have invited Marc and Dee. Darius might be spiteful, but he wasn't hateful. No, he simply planned to bed her.

The problem was he planned to bed her not out of desire, although she didn't doubt he still wanted her, but out of some misguided need for domination. Which meant that regardless of her recent revelation, she had to remain a reluctant participant. In other words, no jumping into his bed at the first glance. After all, an eager victim was no victim at all, and Darius was just smart enough to see through that.

No, she had to play it cool and make him work for it. She nodded to herself, satisfied with her recent discovery. Suddenly, she was anxiously looking forward to their little family vacation.

She climbed out of the car and headed to the dry cleaner when the sign on the business next door caught her eye. Clippers Beauty Salon. Struck by inspiration, Liz suddenly knew the perfect way to convey her so-called defiance. *Time for a new look.* She turned and headed into the beauty salon.

# Chapter 11

"Is the bungalow ready?" Darius paced the lobby of his hotel awaiting his arriving guests, as nervous as a boy going on his first date. It had been exactly three months since he'd returned to New Zealand, but it felt more like a year since he'd last seen Liz and Marc.

"Yes, boss, everything is prepared."

"The flowers?"

"Yes, boss, fresh flowers in every room."

"The gift baskets?"

"Yes, three baskets. One filled with fruit and chocolates, one filled with quilting supplies, and the third filled with toys."

"*Knitting* supplies—one should be filled with knitting supplies. Make sure it's correct."

"Yes, boss."

"What about that other little errand?"

Alika's shy glance slid away quickly and Darius was certain he saw a quick blush darken his assistant's tanned skin. "Yes, it's all tucked in your closet, just as you asked."

"Alika, what would I do without you?"

"We'll never have to know, will we, boss?"

"No, we won't."

Darius paced to the window once more, looking for the bright-orange courtesy van that picked up guests from the nearby airport. "What about the luau tonight, is everything set?"

"Of course. I've been planning luaus for over two years now. I know *exactly* how you like it."

Darius glanced back, noting the slightly annoyed tone of Alika's voice. "And you do a wonderful job. Sorry for doubting you."

Alika's face relaxed, and he seemed slightly appeased by the apology. "I'll go check on the *knitting* basket." The lanky younger man turned and loped off through the glass sliding doors leading to the bungalows.

Darius paced back to the front counter and back across the presently empty lobby, glad to have the rare solitude. From the moment he had checked out of the hospital in Cleveland, the plans for this week had been running through his mind.

How differently things had worked out from what he'd first expected. When he'd first made this bargain, he'd done so with the intention of this being a week of revenge. A chance to give Liz a little taste of the humiliation she'd heaped on him all those years ago.

Instead, this week had become his last, his only chance to make things right between them. This week had become his chance to reclaim the family that was always meant to be his. There could be no mistakes this week.

He crossed back to the front bay windows as he heard the low familiar rumble of the courtesy van pulling up in front of the hotel lobby. His already accelerated heart seemed to skip a beat as the driver opened the double doors to allow the guests to exit.

As the barrage of people poured out onto the flower-lined walkway, his eyes searched the group for just one. And he spotted her right away, dressed in a bright-yellow halter-necked jumpsuit that hugged her slender waist before flaring out at the legs. Her small feet were encased in beige sandals that revealed her bright-red-painted toes.

His eyes traveled back up, savoring every ounce of her elegant beauty. Her brown eyes were covered by dark shades…and then suddenly his heart completely stopped. Not believing what he was seeing, his eyes widened in surprise and then narrowed in understanding.

Apparently, he wasn't the only one who had thought this trip was about revenge. Gone were the long, lush locks she'd worn ever since the day he met her. Her midnight-black tresses had been shorn into an almost boyish cut. The back was shaped close to her head leaving a short lock over her forehead. Despite her effort, the cut did nothing to reduce her beauty, but still…he'd spent many nights imagining his fingers tangled in her hair as he held her in his arms.

Suddenly, a small shadow darted out from behind her, and Darius's attention was immediately shifted as Marc moved around his mother to get a better look at the place. As usual, the boy was closely followed by his own shadow, as Dee pulled up the rear of the small group.

The guests began filing into the lobby, and Darius was forced to smile and greet them as they went to check in. Liz was climbing the stairs when their eyes connected, and a small smile of satisfaction curved her lips as she watched him examine her hair cut.

"Uncle Darius!" Marc spotted him and hurried up the stairs to meet him.

Darius scooped him up in his arms and the momentum swung them both in a circle. He squeezed his son tightly against his chest, only now realizing how much he'd missed holding the small warm body, so vibrantly alive. He closed his eyes against the tears, knowing how easily the operation could've gone wrong. How easily he could've been denied this small privilege.

Dee gave them both a brief hug. "Darius, this is beautiful."

He smiled, unable to hide the pride he felt in his hotel. "Thank you. Welcome to the Hawaiki Inn." His eyes slid back to Liz, where she stood with her arms crossed over her chest, still smiling.

"Nice haircut."

Her smile spread to a grin. "Thanks, I like it."

"Well, I don't," Dee interrupted with a shake of her head. "Don't know what that girl was thinking, cutting off all her beautiful hair."

Darius knew exactly what she was thinking, but kept it to himself. He glanced back to be sure someone was tending the desk, and saw one of the staff was taking care of the long line of guests. "I know you're probably tired from that long trip, so how about I show you to your bungalow." He opened the glass door leading to the front desk. "Don't worry about checking in, that's all been taken care of, I have your keys right here." He handed Dee the key.

Liz noticed the action, but said nothing.

"Uncle Darius, do you think we'll see any dolphins while we're here?" Marc asked, skipping up beside him.

"I think you just might."

"What's that?" Marc asked, and slipping his hand into Darius's much larger one he pointed to the small red-and-purple bird sitting on the branch of a nearby fern tree.

"That's a crimson rosella. Pretty, huh?" Darius asked, realizing with satisfaction that for every experience he'd missed in his son's life there were still hundreds of things left to teach him. Thousands of experiences left to share.

"Yeah—is all this yours?" Marc looked around the bungalow village in awe.

"Sure is. How about tomorrow I give you all a full tour?" Darius asked no one in particular, as he guided them down the bricked covered walkway.

"That's a great idea, isn't it, Mom?" Marc glanced back at his mother.

Liz forced a tight smile. "Just great."

"And tonight, we have a luau." Darius turned down a separate path leading to a bungalow set off by itself.

"What's a luau?" Marc asked, his eyes darting in every direction as he attempted to take in everything.

"It's sorta like a party—but Hawaiian style." He slid the master card key into the door slot. "Here we are."

Darius opened the door and swung it wide, and watched with satisfaction as Marc's and Dee's eyes lit up like children on Christmas morning, but Liz's reaction was even more telling. She glanced at the suite's interior and then back at Darius with a question in her eyes.

The elegant suite was decorated in soft earth tones, everything from the muted beige walls to the plush dark brown carpeting that you literally sank into. The forest-green chenille sofa and matching oversize chairs that screamed comfort and luxury were the perfect companions to the frosted glass coffee and end tables.

On the opposite side of the hexagon-shaped room sat a rectangular, wood dining table with seating for eight. The light wood surface was polished to a high shine, reflecting the large bouquet of tropical flowers that sat in the center of it.

Darius fought the urge to smile. She was right where he wanted her. Confused.

Marc rushed into the room and straight to the large basket sitting on the long dining table. "Cool!" he picked it up and carried it to the couch. "Is this for me?" He asked the question more out of formality than any real doubt.

"Yes, it is." Darius answered, but the boy was already tearing the cellophane wrapping apart.

Liz moved a step closer to him, and spoke so only he could hear her. "This is nothing like the bungalow I stayed in before."

"This is the VIP suite." He suddenly slipped his arm around her waist and felt her whole body tense in surprise. "That haircut is really sexy on you, gives a man easy access to your soft neck."

He leaned down as if to kiss her neck, and Liz shifted out of his hold and quickly moved across the room without another word between them. By then, Dee had found her basket, and she turned and looked at Darius with such gratitude in her eyes he felt a little bad that he hadn't thought to give her something more impressive than a basket of knitting supplies.

"This is lovely," Dee said, holding the basket up to see everything inside.

"Look, Mom." Marc held up a remote-control airplane. "Uncle Darius, let's go fly it!"

"Not right now," Liz held up her hands to halt Marc's sprint to the front door. "Maybe later." Liz glanced around the room, mesmerized by the elegance of it. She saw the suite had four adjoining doors that she would later discover led to three separate bedrooms, each with its own private bathroom and to a kitchen. "I'm sure Darius has a lot to do with new guests checking in."

She stood with her back to him talking only to Marc, and he knew he was being dismissed. "Actually, I was hoping I could have a word alone with you, Liz."

She turned in surprise. "Oh?"

Darius wasn't buying her surprise for a moment. If she wanted him to spell it out, he would. "Yes, about the agreement—"

"Oh, yes! That!" She hurried over and pushed him toward the door. "I'll be right back, Dee." She pushed him through the door and closed it behind her. "Have you lost your mind?! How dare you mention *that* in front of my aunt and son?"

"Mention what?"

Her brown eyes narrowed. "The bargain." She hissed between her teeth.

Darius turned and started slowly down the walk away from the bungalow. "What are you so upset about? The bargain was that you would return and spend seven days with me here." He gestured to the flower gardens surrounding them on all sides. "Seven days in paradise doesn't sound like too bad a bargain."

"It's more than that and you know it."

"Do I?" He rubbed his chin thoughtfully. "I don't recall our ever discussing any specifics."

"We didn't have to—you made it perfectly clear what you wanted."

"Did I?"

Walking fast, she easily caught up with him. "*Yes, you did.*"

The pair walked in silence for a few seconds until they reached the white, scrolled iron fence that lined the cliff edge. Darius turned and leaned his hip against it. "So, refresh my memory. What is it I expect again?"

Liz's eyes flashed fury for a brief second and then it was gone. "Nice try. If you want to embarrass me, you're going to have to do better than that."

"Liz, all I want is to spend some time with you and my son. Is that too much to ask?"

She moved to stand beside him at the railing looking out over the deep-blue harbor. "That's all?"

"That's all."

"When I left here back in January…that wasn't all." She turned to look at his profile. "So, what changed?"

"I found out I have a son." He looked directly into her eyes. "A discovery like that tends to change a man's priorities."

"Darius, I'd rather know up front…if there are strings attached."

"I told you before—I don't take anything that is not offered."

She just continued to stare at him. "You're the most chameleon-like human being I've ever met. Every time I think I have you all figured out, you change."

"So? Friends?"

"I guess so."

He shook his head with a laugh. "That's a start."

He turned to face the harbor as the cool afternoon

breeze floated by carrying the fragrant scent of flowers. His smile faded, as a thought occurred to him. "Marc still thinks I'm his uncle."

"I know." She glanced at him and quickly looked away.

"When are you going to tell him the truth?"

"I need some time, Darius."

"You've had three months."

"Look, I've made a mess of this whole situation from the moment he was conceived. I know that now. All I'm asking is that you give me a little time to make it right. Can you do that?"

"Yes." He sighed heavily. "But understand, Liz, I don't plan to be Uncle Darius forever." A few minutes later he walked her back to the bungalow. "See you at the luau tonight." Lifting her chin with his index finger he looked directly into her eyes. "It's important to me that you have a good time this week. So, feel no pressure. You don't have to do anything you don't want to. Okay?"

She smiled, and he sensed her relief. "Okay."

He gave her a little peck on the forehead and started back down the walkway, feeling better than he had in weeks, never noticing the frown that followed him, or the soft "damn" that floated by on a breeze.

# Chapter 12

So, *now* he wanted to be friends. *Fickle man!*

As she dressed for the luau later that evening, all Liz could think about was Darius. All the Dariuses she'd met over a lifetime. The young, ambition-driven Darius who'd assumed his whole life would fall into place because he deemed it so. The stable, seemingly boring one of her youth. The angry resentful Darius she'd met upon arriving in New Zealand the first time, the Darius who wanted nothing more than to cause her the same amount of shame and humiliation he felt she'd given him. And then there was Darius, the doting father and forgiving friend who seemed to have somehow shaken free of both those other past personae.

If only she could do so as easily, Liz thought. But the memory of her past was there every time she heard her son refer to his father as his uncle. Her past was there every time she instinctively reached to touch Darius before remembering to pull back. It seemed the more time she spent with him, the more it felt as if they'd never been apart. He was starting to feel familiar again, and that was not good. This was supposed to be nothing more than a fling, and she had to remember that first and foremost. Of course, if he kept insisting on not taking what wasn't offered it might not even be that.

A short knock on her door brought her back to the present. "Come in."

Dee poked her head around the door. "Just wondering if you were close to ready, Marc is as anxious as a puppy to get down to the beach."

As Liz glanced in the full-length mirror she remembered the last luau she'd attended here and wondered if she could stir Darius's male senses likes that again.

"Oh, my." Dee came into the room with wide eyes, taking in the strapless, black knit dress that hugged her niece's body like a glove from breast to hip. The dress was cut at an angle from thigh to the ankle. Between the open-knit design and the side slit, more than a little of her bronze skin was revealed to any prying eyes.

"I bought it right before we left Columbus." Liz bit her lip in preparation for Dee's trademark honesty. "What do you think?"

A wide grin came across Dee's face. "I think he doesn't stand a chance." With that she darted out the door.

Liz stood staring at the mirror. "I sure hope not."

As the trio came to the top of the brick stairs leading down to the beach, Dee stopped. "My Lord," she said in awe, looking out over the cliff top where the burnished sun appeared to be literally sitting down on top of the deep-blue harbor. "His majesty never ceases to amaze me."

Liz smiled, knowing exactly how her aunt felt. It was the same way she'd felt when she'd first set eyes on the harbor. "Darius once told me that he doesn't understand why people move away from here."

Dee glanced at Liz. "What a beautiful place to call home."

Marc, not the least bit impressed by the sunset, was too busy watching the activity on the beach as the costumed dancers swayed their hips and arms to the steady drum beats. In the distance he could see a bunch of children gathered around the inflatable buildings. "Come on, it's already started." He moved to go down the stairs ahead of the two women.

"Marc, be careful," Liz called after him, but relaxed when she saw Darius move away from the crowd coming in their direction, knowing he would meet Marc at the bottom. Slowly, Liz made her own way down the steep stairs, allowing her aunt to brace herself on her shoulder.

Darius drew closer and lifted his arm to wave in greeting, but the wave was stopped in midflight as his eyes fell on Liz. She continued to lead Dee down the stairs, trying to pretend the arrow had not hit the target.

"What are they doing?" Marc asked, pointing to the dancers as he wrapped himself around Darius's waist. The boy's narrow little arms were crinkling the delicate material of his white linen tunic, but Darius didn't seem to notice.

"Dancing, but not just any dance. Their dance has a message in it." He spoke to his son, but Darius's eyes were still firmly fixed on Liz as she and Dee finally reached the bottom.

"Darius, I have to say again, what a lovely place you

have here." Dee beamed up at him. "Do you hold a luau every week?"

He glanced at Dee but his eyes quickly returned to Liz. "Thank you, Dee. Yes, the weekly luau is one of our guests' favorite activities ." He took Liz's hand, lifting her arm to get a better look at the dress. "You look lovely."

"Thank you." Liz could not stop the smile that spread across her face. "Looks like a good crowd tonight."

As if only then remembering the crowd of noisy people behind him, Darius turned. "Yes, the hotel is fully booked."

Marc took Darius's hand from his mother's and started pulling him toward the luau. "Come on, Uncle Darius, I wanna see."

"Okay, okay." Darius laughed as he allowed himself to be dragged away. "Come on, ladies, there is plenty to eat and drink," he called back to Liz and Dee.

Liz watched her son pull his father into the thick of the crowd and the guests parted, making room for them. She watched as Darius made conversation with his guests easily, and realized once again how naturally suited to this lifestyle he seemed to be.

Never would she have imagined that the ambitious boy working hard to build his deli and supermarket empire would end up running a vacation resort on the other side of the world. But, then again, her life hadn't turned out exactly as planned either.

As they approached the group, the wait staff drifting almost unseen through the crowd appeared occasionally, offering up trays of various chicken dishes, one called katsu, which to Liz just looked like fried chicken with some kind of sauce over it. Then another tray of char siu, which translated to spareribs, and various other chicken, fish and pork dishes. There were tray after tray of side dishes, rice, salad and even chowders.

Liz rejected offering after offering and just shook her head at the sheer multitude of things available. At the other end of the grouping, opposite the dancers was a long bar and a bartender whom the hotel guests were keeping busy. Not to mention that trays of colorful drinks were also circulating throughout the crowd. Darius wasn't joking when he said there would be plenty to eat and drink.

As nervous as her stomach was, Liz was afraid to eat anything, but that did not stop Dee from sampling pretty much everything that came by them. Marc and Darius had worked their way to the front and she could see Darius gesturing to the dancers and talking to Marc, who watched the dancers with rapt attention. In fact, Marc was watching the dancers' rapidly rotating hips with such rapt attention she began to wonder exactly at what age testosterone began to kick in.

"Hello."

Liz jumped, slightly startled, as a smiling young man appeared at her side. "Hello." She smiled in return.

"My name is Alika. I am Mr. North's personal assistant. I just wanted to introduce myself and let you know that as Mr. North's special guest, if you need anything, anything at all, just let me know. Twenty-four hours a day I am at your disposal."

Liz's eyes darted to Darius who was still engrossed in his dance lesson with Marc. "Um, thank you. But, I'm sure that won't be necessary."

Alika help up a hand to still her refusal. "Truly, it is my privilege. I take care of all Mr. North's special guests."

Liz's perfectly arched eyebrow lifted as a thought

occurred to her. "Does Mr. North have special guests often?"

"Oh, yes, quiet often. Almost every week."

The other eyebrow lifted. "Oh, really?"

Alika frowned, confused, and then his brown eyes widened suddenly. "Oh, no, no—I meant businessmen and important officials. Not—not, guests like you."

Liz wanted to ask exactly what kind of guest Alika thought she was, but didn't want to get her feelings hurt. "Well, thank you, I appreciate the offer. But I will try not to impose on you any more than necessary."

Alike smiled broadly and Liz realized for the first time how very young and handsome he was. And she realized she'd seen him before, on her last visit to the island.

"Whatever you need, please do not hesitate to call on me. Enjoy the rest of your evening." He made a small nod to Liz and then to Dee before moving off through the crowd.

"Darius is certainly going out of his way to make sure we're taken care of," Dee said, taking a sampling of salmon off a passing tray.

"Yes, he is," Liz agreed as she watched Darius guide Marc to a group of children playing on the nearby inflatable slides. Darius introduced Marc to the other children and before long they'd all disappeared inside one of the bouncers.

"Excuse me?" An older woman with a local accent approached Dee. "Can I ask you how that tastes?"

"Delicious," Dee said, quickly wiping her mouth with a small napkin that came with the salmon.

"Not too spicy?"

"No, just right."

"Oh, good, good. I wanted to sample it. But I have

an ulcer, you know. Can't just go putting anything in the old stomach, now can I?"

"No, I don't suppose you should," Dee agreed. "Oh, here he comes again."

The waiter carrying the salmon came upon them just then and the stranger stopped him, and examined his tray carefully, before picking up a small piece. "Think I'll start with this little fellow."

Dee took the opportunity to help herself to another piece, and the two women, equal in age and stature, were nibbling away at the fish when an older man joined them.

"I'm Fiona McKinsey," the woman said. "And this is my husband, Larry."

Larry pulled off a piece of his wife's fish. "Surprised to see you trying this," he commented to his wife.

"This nice lady here suggested it," Fiona said, "and she was right." Fiona chuckled before tossing the last bit in her mouth.

Dee wiped her hand before extending it to the couple. "I'm Delia Donovan and this is my niece Elizabeth."

"Nice to meet you." Liz managed to pull her attention away from Darius and Marc long enough to be introduced to the couple.

"We have a table right over there, with a couple of empty seats if you would like to join us," Fiona offered. "I love these luaus but they are murder on the feet."

"I know exactly what you mean and I only just arrived," Dee answered and the two women fell into a fit of laughter.

Larry gestured in the direction of the table and stood back to allow the three women to pass, Fiona leading the way. Just as the small round table came into sight, Liz found herself stopped by a large hand wrapped around her waist.

"Mind if I steal this one, Larry?" Darius's deep voice came from over her head.

Larry chuckled. "I guess I'll just have to settle with these two lovelies."

"Come along, dear." Fiona continued to lead the small group to the table, leaving Liz and Darius standing on the edge of the luau.

"Can we take a walk?" he asked.

"In the dark?"

"It's not dark yet." He took her arm, leading her away down the deserted beach. "Besides, we have the moon to guide the way."

As they walked along, Liz glanced back over her shoulder to see Marc being chased by another little boy and laughing loudly.

"Don't worry, he's perfectly safe." He stopped and turned her back toward the large group. "See those guys there, there and there." He pointed to a triangle of points around the crowd. "Those are my employees, and their sole purpose is to watch over the guests. Make sure no one gets out of hand, or gets drunk and wanders out into the water, or the children get into any mischief."

"Mischief? I don't know what you're talking about, my baby is an angel."

He huffed. "He's my son, remember? Try that on someone else."

She laughed. "Okay, but he *is* well-behaved."

"When you're around."

Liz glanced down and realized they were holding hands, but she said nothing. Looking up at the bright lights that lit up the night sky, she said, "It's amazing how clearly you can see the stars from here."

"Why not? There is nothing out here to disrupt the view." He sighed. "Many nights I've lain out on the beach just counting the constellations." He pointed. "Big Dipper, Little Dipper."

She pointed to another. "What's that?"

He frowned up at the star grouping. "Medium Dipper?"

She laughed. "I'm no astrologist, but I'm pretty sure there is no *Medium* Dipper."

"Sure there is." he said, with a small smile forming on his lips.

"Um…no."

He pointed to another. "See, it's right next to Super-Size Dipper."

"There is *definitely* no Super-Size Dipper."

He tilted his head and looked at her with a slightly confused expression. "Really?"

Liz smiled and shook her head. "It's a good thing you're cute."

Darius laughed. "Thanks, I think." They walked along in silence for a moment, before Liz asked to stop to remove her sandals.

"Do you remember why we chose New Zealand for our honeymoon?" Darius asked, while he waited for her.

Liz stood straight and avoided eye contact. "We didn't decide on New Zealand, Darius. You chose it, remember?"

Darius's face shifted to denial and then a blank expression came over it. "Right, I forgot." He huffed again. "Somehow I had gotten it into my head that we chose this place together. But now I remember. It was recommended by the travel agent."

Liz glanced around the serene setting. From there the music from the luau was reduced to background noise, and even the laughter and commotion from the guests were dim murmurs. "Well, you couldn't have chosen a better place," Liz said, trying to regain the easy mood they'd shared just moments ago. "It's beautiful here, I understand why you stayed." She looked back at him and found Darius's eyes trained on her body. "What?"

He shook his head as if coming out of a trance. "Nothing. You look fabulous in that dress. I never would've imagined you in something like that?"

"Like what?"

"Provocative."

She smiled slyly. "Am I provoking you, Darius?"

His eyes narrowed on her face. "Are you trying to?"

Liz felt her heart skip a beat, and she quickly turned away. "What do you mean, you never would've imagined me in something like this?"

"It's just, you use to be such a proper little thing."

"Proper? What's that supposed to mean?"

He laughed at her outrage. "Sorry, but you were…kind of a Barbie doll. Or, at least I thought you were. But I see now I was wrong. You're a lot tougher than I ever gave you credit for being, Liz."

The look of admiration in his eyes caused her heart to skip a beat. She shrugged. "A person is as tough as they have to be."

"No, not everyone holds up under pressure, but you did. Not only did you hold up, you managed to get some pretty impressive things accomplished. Getting your degree and raising such a wonderful kid at the same time is no easy task."

"I had Dee."

"I know, but still. I'm impressed by your determination."

She turned away to keep from blushing like a schoolgirl. "Will you please stop complimenting me, I'm not used to it."

He laughed. "From me? Or just in general?"

"Both."

"Come on, I used to compliment you…didn't I?"

She moved toward the water. "Of course, you did, I'm just joking." She stopped as a soft wave of cool water rolled over her feet.

A few seconds later, Darius came to stand beside her. "No, you weren't."

She glanced at him. "Of course I was. You use to compliment me all the time."

"No, I didn't. I remember how it was back then, Liz. Compliments weren't really my thing. Like everything else, I just assumed you knew how I felt." He ran his hand over the back of her short haircut, letting his fingers slide along her jawline. "I never told you how much I loved your thick, beautiful hair and how I enjoyed tangling my fingers in it when we made love." He turned to face her and the water covered his sandaled feet, but he didn't seem to notice. His complete attention was on her eyes. He stared so deep, Liz wondered if he were seeking a way into her soul. "I never told you how beautiful you are, or how lucky I felt I was to have you. I never told you how much I loved you, or how much I was looking forward to our life together."

"Darius, don't say that. Not now, not here—when it's too late to make a difference." Liz shook her head and started to back away.

But he reached out and cupped her face in his large palms. "Is it too late, Liz?"

She lifted her eyes to his and felt her heart melting

in her chest at the depth of emotion she saw there. "I don't know."

He smiled. Not a conquering smile, but one of understanding. "Then let me help you decide."

# *Chapter 13*

Darius leaned forward and touched his warm mouth to hers in a soft brushing of the lips initially, but then Liz felt his hot tongue slide across her bottom lip, exploring, remembering, and all she could do was stand frozen in time and pray that the perfect moment never ended.

She felt his large hand grip her jaw more firmly, but gently, as his other arm slipped around her waist, pulling her closer to his body. Her own tongue reached for his.

It had been so long since she'd been held by him, for all that she remembered, so much had been forgotten. The strength in his arms, the changing of rhythm as his heartbeat matched itself to hers, the feel of his growing erection throbbing against her stomach, making promises she knew he could keep.

Liz felt her own arms lifting to wrap around his neck, wanting to hold him like this forever. The textured feel of the knit fabric of her dress against his linen tunic and slacks only added to the sensuality building throughout her whole body.

How could she ever have walked away from this? He was so warm and alive, and even after all these years and all the damn confusion he still felt more right than anything. How was that possible? Hearing the soft sigh that escaped from her throat, Liz decided she didn't care how, she was just glad for it.

Holding her against his chest, Darius thought she smelled as sweet and fresh as the island flowers. His hands roamed over the outline of her body, made so conveniently available by the open material of the dress.

His mouth moved to her bare neck and he found that he liked the short haircut after all, because, just as he'd told her, it gave him easy access to the soft skin of her neck. "Come back to my bungalow with me," he whispered against her ear, right before she heard another sound coming from further down the beach.

"Mom! Mom!"

Liz turned to find Marc being followed by a long line of children and they were all headed directly for her and Darius.

Darius came up behind her, pressing his hard erection against her soft bottom. "Is it too late, Liz?"

Liz was torn between the feel of the warm body against her and her child calling for her attention. "What?"

"Quick, before they get here, just answer the question. Is it too late?"

"No," she whispered.

He quickly moved away from her. Kicking off his sandals, he moved toward the water until it reached his thighs, and then he dove in. Liz watched in amazement as he swam out into the harbor, her mind scrambled and confused.

By then, Marc and his friends had caught up to her. He stopped, his chest puffing with exertion. "What you doing down here?"

Liz looked at her son, trying to hide her slight annoyance that this simple question was apparently the big emergency that had broken up their sweet interlude. "Just talking to Darius." She looked back out toward the water, somewhat fearful for his safety, but this was his home so she could only assume he knew what he was doing.

"What's Uncle Darius doing?" Marc asked.

"Just taking a swim." She turned to the other children, eager to get her curious child's mind off the current topic. "So, who are your friends?"

Marc proceeded to introduce the trio of children that had followed him. Liz wasn't sure if she should leave Darius to his swim or not, but after a few minutes without him returning, she decided to lead the children back to the luau, each of them trying to tell her everything they'd seen and done in the time they'd been there and constantly talking over each other. Liz smiled to herself, taking comfort in the familiarity of being surrounded by chattering children. Soon, she was feeling like her old self again, and the closer they came to the luau the more the kiss with Darius felt like a sweet dream. By the time they reached the table where Dee was sitting with the McKinseys the children had peeled away once again.

Another older couple had joined Dee and the McKinseys and they were all laughing and talking as if they'd known each other for years.

Dee glanced up at Liz when she saw her approaching the table. "There you are. Having a good time?"

Liz smiled and nodded, but Dee's frown told her she hadn't hidden her confusion as well as she'd hoped.

"Everything okay?" Dee asked.

She nodded again. "I'm just a little tired, think I'll turn in."

Dee leaned to the side to look around her. "Where's Darius?"

"He went for a swim."

"A swim? In the dark?"

Liz's mouth twisted. "That's what I thought."

"The water is still quiet tolerable even in the evening hours," Fiona added to the conversation. "I've been known to indulge in the occasional late-night dunking myself."

Dee frowned at her new friend. "Well, you won't catch me out there in the dark. Who knows what's under that water."

Fiona laughed. "This close to shore, Dee, nothing more troubling than the occasional koi."

"I don't want to spoil his fun," Liz interrupted the arguing women. "But can you bring Marc in when you come, Aunt Dee?"

"Of course." Dee reached out and touched her arm. "You sure everything is okay?"

Liz forced a bright smile. "Yes, I'm just not used to all this activity." She waved at the group. "Good night everyone."

"Good night, Liz," the McKinseys called out.

"Sleep well, dear," Dee called after her.

Liz started across the sand to the stairs leading back up to the hotel bungalows, and was quickly intercepted by Alika.

"Everything okay, miss?"

She smiled. "Yes, everything is wonderful. I'm just turning in for the night."

He glanced back at the luau. "But the party is now in full swing."

Liz reflected for a moment that Alika's willingness to be helpful could quickly become annoying. "Not for me. Good night."

She climbed the stairs, removing her hoop earrings as she went. By the time she reached the top, she was near exhaustion.

She stopped at the top to look back out over the harbor, but by now the night sky was pitch-black except for the bright stars. She searched down beach but found no sign of movement in the water. For a brief second, she considered the worst possible conclusion and her heart stopped in her chest, but then she remembered that Darius had been living on the island for close to ten years and knew the harbor far better than she did.

She turned and started down the path to her bungalow. Feeling a slight chill on the air, she wrapped her arms around her body, remembering the feeling of being in Darius's embrace and wondering if it would happen again.

Earlier that day, he'd given her the impression that friendship was all he was interested in, and for a while she'd been disappointed that her island fling would never happen. But now she was even more worried, because the feel of being held by him again let her know that no matter what she told herself, Darius would never be a fling for her. He was the love of her life, and she'd broken his heart.

She came to her bungalow and paused at the door, remembering Darius had given Dee the room key earlier. She slumped against the door and considered going back down to the beach to get it from Dee, but then she glanced in the other direction and realized the lobby was closer.

"Can't get in?" The deeply mellow voice came out of the darkness.

"Darius? Is that you?"

"Yeah, it's me." He moved from behind a tree and for the first time Liz heard the shiver in his voice. He moved toward her and Liz noticed his wet clothes were clinging to his body. "Here, I'll let you in."

As he moved past her, she was surprised by the heat radiating from his body beneath the wet clothes. She grabbled his wet tunic as he moved to open the door. "Darius…" She looked up at him, pleading with her eyes.

He leaned forward and placed a gentle kiss on her forehead. "Yeah, I know." He kissed her again, and chuckled. "So far this week is nothing like I thought it would be."

"What did you think it would be?"

"I wanted to show you I was not the man I used to be." He started to reach out to her, but held back. "You deserve a man who can appreciate you, Liz, I want to be that man."

She frowned. "What are you talking about? I'm the one who betrayed you."

"Shh." He placed his lips against her, at the same time opening the door to the suite. He led her inside and to her private room. Once they were both inside he locked the door from the inside and leaned his back against it.

"Damn." His hungry eyes roamed over her slender body. "That dress has been driving me crazy all night. I've been dying to see you in the light."

She smiled and turned in a slow circle, lifting her arms behind her head. "Well, here I am."

In a flash he was across the room and had her wrapped in his arms. "And all night I've been thinking about taking it off you."

His mouth went to her breast and he removed the thin material with his teeth, sliding it down her body, kissing his way along the path he was creating.

Liz felt as if her whole world was spinning on its axis as he lifted her in his arms to carry her to the bed. "Wait! What about Dee and Marc?"

He laid her on the bed and began pulling his wet tunic over his head. "What about them?"

"What if they come in and hear us?" Liz was trying to focus, but it was hard when all his sun-gold skin was being revealed, inch by beautiful inch.

A gorgeous smile spread across his face. "Then I guess you're gonna have to keep it down, huh?" He stretched out on the bed beside her. "If I remember right, you're a screamer."

"Am not."

He flipped over on his back and began unsnapping his slacks. "We'll see about that."

Liz propped herself up on one elbow to watch the show as he removed his slacks and underwear. He struggled to slide the wet material down over his narrow hips and Liz held her breath as she waited for his manhood to be revealed.

But suddenly he stopped and looked at her.

"What?" she asked, fearing he'd once again changed his mind.

"Come with me." He stood and, taking her hand, lifted her from the bed. He led her into the bathroom and closed the door. He turned to the tub and Liz noticed for the first time that it had a built-in whirlpool.

She watched fascinated as he started the bath, checking and double-checking the temperature before adding some nearby bath crystals that soon had the tub filling with suds and bubbles. He definitely had something in mind and she couldn't wait to see exactly what it was.

Once he was satisfied with the progress on the bath, he turned back to her. "I've waited for this too long to hurry. I want us to take our time and enjoy each other." He moved closer to her and took her in his arms once more.

Liz felt the same way, but the sensible part of her was still concerned about the return of her family. Until she decided how to tell Marc the truth, she did not want him to know they were intimate.

His soft mouth found hers and Liz was once again struck by the electrical charge that seemed to race through her body whenever he touched her. Every time he wrapped his arms around her she felt suddenly safe and cocooned in a way she hadn't felt in years. In a way she was afraid to get attached to.

Despite the moment, the future was still too uncertain to risk her heart. He stepped back and finally removed his wet slacks and underwear, and Liz was once again struck by his masculine beauty.

His entire body was such a rich, dark golden brown except from his thighs to hips, which were just slightly lighter from the protection of swim trunks and shorts. Looking at him now, there was so much she remembered and yet so much seemed new.

She looked up into his soft brown eyes and knew that a part of him would always be the man she'd once known, the man she'd once run from and now realized that a person could never run from their destiny. It would always, always find them.

At the same time, she saw something else in his eyes, a new Darius, formed and molded by this island. A man she'd only met a short while ago, and was still getting to know.

She opened her mouth to ask a question, something that had to be said, but the words could not be formed. Darius looked at her with a slight frown. "I told you before I would not take what wasn't offered. Do you want to be here, Liz?"

How could he think she did not? Liz thought. In answer, she simply stepped back, released the small latch holding her dress on her body and let it fall to the floor. The fire in his eyes as they darkened was proof enough that they both wanted to be here.

Darius turned off the bath and, taking her hand in his, stepped back and into the tub. Liz felt her whole body shivering with anticipation as she joined him inside the sudsy cocoon.

Settling against the back of the tub, Darius lowered her to straddle his hips and Liz immediately recognized the vulnerability of her position.

As if to distract her, he wrapped his arms around her waist and pulled her closer taking her mouth with his. Liz was quickly lost in the sweet taste of his tongue against her, and before long she was the one leading the way as her lips darted to kiss his eyelids and cheeks before returning to his mouth, where he would once again try to regain control of the kiss only to have her dart away to tease him once more.

Finally, his soapy hands came up and held her still as

his tongue plunged inside her mouth, seeking and taking, and Liz felt the kiss all the way to the tips of her toes.

Her body began to move and squirm against his, almost as if it had a mind of its own, and it wanted more, needed more. But Darius held her up, refusing to allow her to settle over his throbbing penis.

"No, baby, let's take it slow this time. I've waited so long for you, Liz." His hungry mouth followed a trail of suds across her chest to her high breast. Lifting the small breast in his hands, his large thumb rolled over the nipple and Liz's back arched as a bolt of lightning shot through her body.

Then he was taking the small breast into his mouth, holding her up as he suckled hungrily. Liz's aching body was almost to the point of desperation. All she wanted was to get him inside her and still he refused.

He lifted his mouth from her breast and looked up into her eyes. "Nothing has ever felt like you." Suddenly, he had taken the other breast into his mouth, and it was everything for Liz not to wrap her arms around his head and hold him to her.

"Darius, I can't take it," she managed to get out between breaths. "I need you so much."

"Shh, it's okay. You have me, baby." But instead of connecting their bodies, he lifted a loofah sponge and dipped it in the water. Lifting it over her head, he let the water run down over her, and the warm water did nothing to cool her urgent need.

He covered the sponge with a liquid soap that smelt of lavender and began sliding it over her arms and shoulders in a slow, rotating fashion that did seem to relax her a bit. One of his large hands came against her back and gently pushed her forward as he did the same to her back. Liz leaned forward, resting her head on his shoulder, and let him have his way.

"Remember this?" he whispered in her ear.

And she did. They'd spent many nights just lounging in the tub together, long after the bathing and loving were done. What a fool she'd been to run from this man.

"Yes," she whispered in return.

"All I ever wanted to do was take care of you, Liz."

She closed her eyes to fight back the tears beginning to form. This was too much, the memories, the emotional connection she felt to Darius, it was all too much. "I know." And she knew, at least now she did.

Eager to fight down some of the intense energy swirling around them, she sat up. "My turn." Taking the loofah from him, she did the same as he had, running it over his arms and shoulders, still fascinated by all the new muscles that now bulged beneath his gold skin.

She dipped the sponge beneath the water to his stomach, slowly moving south, but he quickly covered her hand to stop her. "Um, a loofah is kinda rough for him."

She laughed and placed a quick peck on his lips. "Well, I wouldn't want to do anything to hurt him." Dropping the sponge, she let her fingers roam over the thick erection, as always entranced by the way a man's body changed to suit a woman.

"Liz, I never stopped loving you, you know that, right?" His whispered words were little more than a murmur as his mouth returned to her breast.

Liz bit her lip to keep from blurting her own feelings. She knew that what he was saying was the passion of the moment. How could he love her when he didn't even trust her? But that was a conversation for another place and time, and she was not about to spoil this moment with reality.

"Show me," she whispered back and gasped as she felt his long fingers slide inside her body. Straddling him, she was completely open to his exploration and all she could do was cling to his shoulders as his busy fingers manipulated her flesh, preparing it for his own.

Satisfied she could accept him, Darius lifted her hips slightly and lowered her over the head of his penis. They were both surprised by her tightness as he gently, but determinedly prodded his way inside her body.

Liz could no longer control her breathing as she felt every inch of him enter her—every throb, every vein, every little movement, until it felt she could not be stretched any further and then she was stretched more. Darius's arms came up to her shoulders and with one hard push he was seated inside her.

Liz felt the difference in his body immediately as he stiffened, trying to hold back the tide of hunger pushing them both to finish the act. Liz searched for his mouth, wanting to be as close to him as humanly possible. She'd forgotten this sensation, this feeling unique to womanhood. The strange sense of both power and weakness that came with having a man inside her body.

She continued to kiss him, sensing his will as part of her own to make the moment last, but with every touch of their lips his penis thumped against her vaginal walls until she wanted to cry out at the sensation.

Liz knew they'd lost the battle when Darius wrapped his large hands around her waist and lifted her to slide down on him again. He lifted her again and again, bringing her down on his aching erection wanting, no, desperate for relief.

She watched in fascination as his head fell back against the tub and a look of pure ecstasy came across his face. His whole being became centered and focused on the task of pushing into her body. Liz held to his shoulders as her own eyes closed and she gave way to the building wave coursing through her body like a tsunami rushing to crash against the land.

Liz was unconscious of her fingers digging into his shoulders as the wave reached its destination and her whole being erupted in uncontrolled pulsations. Darius pulled her even closer to him as he followed her into the abyss, pushing into her body with one final thrust, sending his seed deep inside her.

# Chapter 14

For a moment it seemed as if time had stopped. The only sounds that could be heard were the faint sounds of the luau band and their own breathing.

Darius dug around in the water until he found the loofah and once again let the water roll over her face and body. "Told you so."

"What?" she murmured, feeling the aftereffects of their lovemaking, the exhaustion that quickly followed.

"I knew you were a screamer."

Liz started to protest immediately and then remembered. Embarrassment colored her whole body, and she was grateful for the protection of Darius's arms to hide in. She sat back to look at him. "You weren't exactly quiet either."

"But I never claimed to be." Beneath the water, his

hand rubbed her hip seductively. "I've already told you, you drive me wild."

"Do I?"

He chuckled. "You need more proof?"

She leaned forward and whispered in his ear. "Maybe."

His eyes widened. "Okay, but you're gonna have to give me a minute. I'm an old man now, not the young buck I use to be."

"What are you talking about? You're only thirty-four."

"Still a big difference from twenty to thirty."

Liz, still seated on his now-limp penis, wiggled slightly and laughed at the feel of it suddenly springing to life once more. "Not from where I sit."

Darius lifted her back and stood from the tub, and Liz's eyes went immediately to his growing erection. He offered his hand to her and she stood and stepped out of the tub, as well.

He quickly had a towel wrapped around her body as he rubbed over her skin. "Are you cold?"

She smiled at him over her shoulder. "How could I be?"

Once he was satisfied with her, Darius turned the towel on himself. Together they walked back into the bedroom and Darius folded back the covers. He turned to her with a wicked smile. "Now, about that proof."

Before she could say a word, he swooped her up in his arms and dropped her on the bed coming down on top of her. Using his arms to cage her in, he propped himself over the top of her. "Now, where was I?" He feigned ignorance. "Oh, yeah, now I remember." His mouth came down on hers and he settled against her body.

"You know, I fully intended to play hard to get," she said, her mouth twisted in resignation. "So much for that."

"Well, if it's any consolation I had no intention of

sleeping with you this week. So we'll just call it even."
His tongue trailed a path along her neck and the valley
between her breasts.

Taking first one and then the other in his large hands,
he squeezed the twin peaks between his fingers
watching as Liz's back arched in reaction.

He continued his path down over her taut stomach,
kissing first her navel and then the tiny pouch that sat
at the bottom of her stomach, the only evidence of child-
birth left on her near-perfect body.

Liz wrapped her arms around his head, enjoying
the feel of his soft lips as anticipation built. She knew
where he was headed and only hoped he did not stop
until he got there.

Suddenly, he was sliding off the edge. "Hang on," he
whispered, and she watched him disappear into the
bathroom, and he soon reappeared holding up a
condom. Without a word, he kneeled between her legs
and she heard the condom wrapper tear. "I came
prepared this time." He reached forward and pulled her
ankles toward him, lifting them over his shoulders.

Liz felt her heartbeat accelerate and tried to control
her breathing, with no luck.

He looked up at her over the length of her body, his
eyes conveying his thoughts more effectively than
words ever could. Liz licked her lips, her mouth going
dry as his warm palm slid up the inside of her thigh. He
followed the path of his fingers with feather-light kisses,
placing then on the inside of each thigh as he climbed
higher and higher.

Every once in a while, he paused and looked up at
her, torturing her, making her need him as much as he
needed her and Liz was powerless to resist. All she

could do was brace herself against the headboard as his hot mouth touched the core of her being.

Showing no mercy, his tongue dove deep inside her, and Liz's whole body jerked in reaction as the impulse to push against his seeking tongue overcame her. Holding to the headboard she mindlessly lifted her hips giving him easier access and he took it. Holding her thighs apart with his arms, he licked and suckled until she was once again screaming out in pleasure, her mind numb to everything but the sensations he was creating inside her.

Just when she thought she could not take any more, he came over her body and slid into her with an ease that convinced her she was designed for him. Made to fit this man and this man alone. He was the only man her body had ever known, and after tonight, she knew no one else could take his place.

Bracing his weight on his elbows, Darius plowed into her body with relentless strokes, pushing her to the limit and beyond. When she thought they'd reached the point of no return, he would suddenly pull back, pull out of her until just the head of his penis remained inside, barely enough to remind her of the agonizing pleasure that awaited her, of the paradise only he could offer.

Then, as the longing began to subside, he would return, allowing her to feel the whole of his large erection, pushing so deep inside her she was force to lift her legs further to accommodate his size.

It wasn't enough for Darius, he shifted their position, lifting one of her legs over his shoulder, and the other around his waist to give him complete access to her. And he took full advantage of the access, pushing into her body with force, causing her to jerk with every stroke of his stiff penis. She was dying a slow, sweet death and Darius's hard erection was showing no sign of being anywhere near done with her.

Liz felt as if her head was spinning as she fought off the climax, wanting to wait for him, wanting to go to that special place together, but it was pointless as her body surrendered to his, giving up her womanly nectar, the prize for his effort. But it wasn't enough, he just continued to plow into her again and again as if he were a being possessed.

Liz looked up at his face to find his head thrown back, the veins in his neck standing in stark relief as the faint sheen of sweat that coated his body glistened in the lights of the room. His handsome face was twisted in concentration. He looked like a tortured soul to her, and all Liz wanted was to provide whatever he needed.

As if sensing her concern, he looked down at her and their eyes locked for several long minutes as he continued to pound into her body. Her eyes questioned, she wanted to know what he needed from her and he understood.

He leaned forward and kissed her hard, his tongue forcing its way inside. He demanded entrance and she gave it. Wrapping his hands around her bottom, he lifted her even further upon his erection and whispered in her ear. "More. I need more."

Liz wasn't sure how much more she could give, but she put her arms around his neck, pressed her body to his and held on, hoping he could find whatever he needed in her.

Still he plowed away at a relentless pace and Liz felt her body renewing itself, finding a way to give him the more he needed. Soon, her juices were once again flowing down to meet his own and together they exploded like two bright stars colliding in the night sky.

\* \* \*

When Liz woke, she found herself alone in the bed. She glanced at the clock on the nightstand and saw that it was almost four in the morning. She felt her nakedness beneath the covers and looked around the room. Everything from clothing to towels had been picked up, her dress was thrown neatly over a nearby chair, and Darius's clothes were gone.

She went to stand from the bed and felt her body immediately reject the notion. She was sore from the tips of her toes to the top of her head, and all she could do was fall back on the pillows and smile at the ceiling. Her mind wandered back over the past evening and she tried to replay every tiny detail. *The drought is over. And what a storm.*

Now knowing what to expect, she attempted to stand again and this time pushed past the stiffness. She needed to get some night clothes on, knowing her son would probably come charging in at the crack of dawn.

Going to the closet she pulled one of her old, worn gowns from the closet and suddenly found it lacking. For the first time in years she wanted something sexy to sleep in, but seeing this was all she had, she slipped the gown over her head and headed to the door.

She went to open the door and realized it was still locked. She frowned down at the handle, wondering how Darius had got out if the door was still locked. She quickly decided that as the owner he probably had a key that could lock it from the other side.

As she stepped out of her room, she realized all was quiet in the bungalow. The lights were all off and the doors to both Dee's room and Marc's were cracked. She peeked into her son's room and smiled to see him sprawled as usual across the bed, every limb pointed in a different direction. The blankets were bunched at the end of the bed. She crossed the room and pulled the blanket over his form, knowing that by morning it would be back at the end of the bed or on the floor. She closed the door and then went to check on Dee, who appeared as just a lump under the covers. For a brief moment, she wondered if they'd seen or heard Darius leaving, but realizing she would not know the answer to that until the next morning, she returned to her bedroom.

She closed the door and leaned back against it, thinking of Darius and all that had happened between them. Much to her dismay, all the girlish hopes and dreams she thought she'd abandoned long ago began to creep into her heart.

She took a deep breath, trying to ground herself in reality. This was a one-week deal. At the end of it, she would return to Columbus and Darius would continue to run his hotel. The only thing that would really change was that now Marc would have his father in his life.

Marc...

She frowned, thinking of just how she was supposed to explain to her son that his uncle was in fact his father, and his father was his uncle. What a mess she'd made of his life. She could only imagine what he would think if he even understood. And as he grew older and did understand, what would he think then?

She ran her hands over her face knowing there was no easy way. She would simply have to tell him and try to answer whatever questions he might have. Liz yawned loudly, and smiled again. She was exhausted, worn out and sore to the core and it all felt so wonderful she wanted to shout. Instead she climbed back into bed, the bed that now smelled faintly of Darius's cologne, wrapped her arms around the pillow where he'd rested his head, took a deep breath and fell right back into a deep sleep.

Darius arrived back at his bungalow a little before four. He tried to lie down and go to sleep, but he was still too wired. He hadn't wanted to leave Liz's bed, but when he awoke a short while ago and realized Dee and Marc were sleeping in the other rooms he knew he had to. The last thing he wanted now was for Liz to be embarrassed in front of her family if they found him in her bed in the morning.

Things were going too good to ruin them now. He crossed to the bar in the corner of his suite and poured himself a short brandy and then walked over to the window that faced the harbor. That was the best sex he'd had in years. He took a sip of the brandy. But then again, it had always been good with Liz. Whatever went wrong between them all those years ago, it hadn't been the sex.

But even better than the sex was the sense that somehow, miracle of miracles, after all the years, after all the pain and confusion of their past, somehow she still felt like his. From the moment he'd held her in his arms all those years ago, so careful and nervous knowing it was her first time and terrified he would hurt her, to the intense, wild lovemaking of tonight, every time he touched her he had the sense that he was the only one.

But that was a lie, and they both knew it. He took another sip of the brandy. It didn't matter, he thought. He was determined to put the pain of the past behind them and start over. They had a son, and that bond was stronger than any she could've ever had with Darren.

With a final sip he finished off the brandy and put the glass on a nearby table. Even now, he wanted nothing more than to go back to her and pick up where they had left off, but they had to be discreet, at least until his son knew the truth.

He turned and headed for his bedroom, thinking of the future and all the things it held for him and Liz. He was already working out the details for her move to New Zealand. He needed to check the local schools and find out about transferring Marc's records here, and the requirements for teachers in case there was some certification Liz needed to teach. Then again, she could always work at the hotel with him. Either way, there was a lot to do, plans to be made and he would get started on them bright and early in the morning.

# Chapter 15

Liz awoke to a heavy weight on her hip bone, and the sound of the television in the background. She yawned and stretched and the dead weight shifted with her.

"Morning, sweetheart," she muttered, burying her head beneath the covers to cling to the last tiny remnant of sleep.

"Morning, Mommy. Hey, did you know they have *SpongeBob* here?"

"No, I did not," she muttered. "Lucky us, huh?"

"Uh-huh, and a lot of other stuff, too." The weight lifted from her hip and Marc's bright, cheerful, fully awake face suddenly appeared over her. "I'm hungry."

She looked up at her son, knowing her respite was now officially over. "Of course you are."

"Can we order room service like they do in the

movies?" His eyes lit up as if ordering room service was some great adventure.

"Why not?" Ignoring her stiff body, Liz sat up in the bed. She reached beside the bed and grabbed the large cloth menu. "Go see if Aunt Dee wants something."

Marc scrambled off the bed and took off into the other room. Liz only shook her head, wondering if she'd ever had that kind of energy. Within two minutes he was back.

Gone was the happy smile, his young face looked solemn. "There is something wrong with Aunt Dee."

Liz was on her feet in an instant and hurrying into the other room. As she approached the bed, she heard her aunt moan. "Aunt Dee? What's wrong?" She tried to pull the covers back to see her aunt's face.

Dee held the covers up. "Nothing, I'm fine."

Liz used her greater strength to slowly peel back the covers. "No, you're not. What's wrong?"

Dee looked up at her sheepishly. "Remember how you told me to go easy on the salmon last night?"

Liz's mouth twisted in understanding. "If I remember right, it wasn't just the salmon. It was the katsu, and the char siu and pretty much anything else that passed you on a tray."

Dee's eyes narrowed on her niece's face. "You don't have to be so smug about it."

Marc was standing beside the bed, his worried eyes going from his mother to his aunt. Liz turned to her son. "Remember when we went to the carnival last year and you ate all that junk food and your tummy hurt?"

He nodded in understanding.

"Well, Aunt Dee ate too much junk food last night."

His brow smoothed in understanding. "Oooh." The

frown reappeared. "Are you gonna have to give her one of those things in her bottom, Mommy?"

Dee's eyes widened. "Say what now?"

Liz laughed. "No, Aunt Dee's a little old for a children's enema. But there are other things we can give her to help."

Liz rested her palm on her aunt's forehead just to assure herself that there was no fever. "I'll call room service and see if they have some kind of antacid tablets."

Dee nodded before burrowing back under the covers. Liz quickly called room service and asked for the antacid tablets as well as breakfast for Marc.

When the breakfast and medicine arrived, they were not brought by room service. Liz just stared in dumbfounded wonder as Darius pushed the cart into the room. Dressed in another of the linen tunics he seemed to favor, today he'd matched it with another pair of long stone-colored safari shorts and black open-toed sandals.

"Morning, Uncle Darius." Marc raced to the man and wrapped himself around his waist as if they hadn't seen each other in years and not just a few hours.

"Morning, champ, I brought your breakfast." He sat the tray of cereal, toast and orange juice on the table before turning to Liz with the bottle of antacid tables. "Everything okay? I heard someone has an upset stomach."

"It's Dee. I'm afraid she enjoyed the luau a little *too* much last night." Liz accepted the bottle from him and went in to give a couple of the tablets to Dee, who gratefully took the chewable tablets and quickly burrowed back under her covers.

A knock on the door caused Liz to turn and Dee to peek out from under her covers. "How are you feeling, Dee?"

"Miserable." She groaned. "You know, there should

be some kind of limit to how much you can eat at a luau, like how much you can drink at a bar before the bartender cuts you off."

Darius chuckled. "Well, the bar was well-watched last night, but I guess I should've kept my eye on the caterers, as well."

"No, it's not your fault, Darius." Liz glanced back at her aunt. "Most people know their own limitations."

"As you can see, I'm not going to get any sympathy from her," Dee grumbled.

"Well, I was coming to get you all for our tour, but I guess that's going to have to wait a couple of days."

Dee shook her head. "No, please, don't let me stop you."

"I'm not going to leave you like this," Liz insisted.

Dee arched an eyebrow at her niece. "No offense, but being alone is better than seeing 'I told you so' in your eyes all day long."

Liz was torn between wanting to spend the day with Darius and caring for her sick aunt. "No, Aunt Dee. Really, I couldn't."

"Please, Darius, help me here. I mean, I love the girl but Florence Nightingale she is not."

"Hey!" Liz frowned at her aunt. "That's mean."

"Look, I'm just going to keep taking these tablets, sleep and let this thing work its way out of my system. There is absolutely no reason why you should sit around here watching that happen."

Liz glanced at Darius who was remaining strangely quiet and found his eyes tracing over the features of her face. She looked backed at Dee. "Are you sure?"

"Absolutely. And if I need anything, I'll just call Mr. Helpful from last night."

"That would be Alika, he's my assistant," Darius added.

Fighting down the guilt of wanting to be with Darius, Liz was still hesitant to leave her sick aunt.

"Darius, can you give us a moment?" Dee said.

He glanced at Liz and then Dee. "Sure." Without another word, he turned and walked back into the living room of the suite.

Dee stretched out her hand and Liz took it as she came closer to the bed.

"Sit." Dee tugged gently.

Liz sat on the side of the bed.

"I appreciate that you want to stay here with me, really I do. But we only have a few days here and you should try to live those days to the fullest." She looked directly into Liz's eyes. "Who knows when you're going to have another opportunity like this, Liz." She glanced toward the doorway.

Liz huffed. "Probably never," she whispered more to herself than Dee.

"Go." Dee leaned forward and placed a soft kiss on her cheek. "Have a good time. And don't worry about me. I'll be fine."

Liz rose from the bed. "Okay, but I have my cell phone if you need me."

"Don't worry about me—go."

A little over an hour later, Alika had been assigned the task of checking on Dee throughout the day, as Darius, Liz and Marc climbed into the Range Rover that would take them around the area on their tour.

"This area is called the Coromandel Peninsula," Darius said, guiding the truck down the driveway away from the resort and onto the main highway. Before long, Liz realized the island was covered not just in beautiful flowers but in lush greenery of every kind. Tall, ancient trees with leaves as green as emeralds hung over the road, shading it from the bright afternoon sun. Within an hour, they'd come to a huge waterfall, and she could only imagine how many gallons of water poured over the huge brown rocks in the course of just one day.

"Can we go swimming in it?" Marc asked.

Liz laughed. "That may not be the best idea, sweetie."

"Definitely not the best idea," Darius seconded.

So instead they stood on the cliff top just enjoying the view. Marc tossed the occasional rock toward the huge waterfall, and then they were off to the coast to catch a ferry to Pauanui Wharf for lunch.

On the ferry ride, Liz was once again struck by the deep blue of the water and the rugged beauty of the surrounding islands. Although most of the local islands were inhabited to some degree, man had yet to leave a mark on the area. In this small corner of the world, nature was still winning the fight.

They stopped at a small restaurant that Darius swore served the best seafood he'd ever had, and after several minutes of deliberation, they ended up trying everything from oysters to squid to blue mackerel.

Later they crossed back over to Tairua Island and Darius explained how Tairua use to be a stand-alone island but was now connected to the mainland by the tiny strip of land that they crossed going back and forth to the hotel resort.

They drove in the Range Rover for little under a half hour until they came to a place called Hahei Beach to swim. Marc raced ahead, eager to get to the water and swim for the first time since arriving. He left the adults to find their own way.

"Marc, be careful," Liz called to his back as he sprinted to the beach.

Marc paused only temporarily as he passed by a huge opening in the side of the mountain. "Uncle Darius, what's that?"

"Cathedral Cove. It's like a mini cave."

"Cool!" For a moment the boy was torn between exploring the cove and swimming, but the blue water won him over and away he went.

"You would never imagine he'd just had major life-changing surgery less than four months ago, would you?" Liz asked with a shake of her head.

Darius smiled at his son as he stopped to collect rocks and twigs. "No, you wouldn't." As they were passing by the cove, Darius stopped Liz, pulling her against his body. He wrapped his arms around her waist. "One night we're coming back here, just you and me, and we're going to make love here."

She smiled seductively. "Promises, promises."

They spent the afternoon swimming in the cool Hahei waters, Darius and Liz mostly avoiding being constantly splashed by Marc who never seemed to tire of the game. By the time they pulled up in front of the hotel later than evening, Marc was sound asleep.

Darius turned off the truck and turned on the seat to face Liz. "Well, I was going to give you a tour of the hotel next, but apparently that's going to have to wait for another day."

"Apparently," she chuckled. "But this was a terrific day, even without the hotel tour. Thanks for taking us around." She glanced back at her sleeping son. "I think I can speak for both of us when I say we had a great time."

"Think you could live here?"

"What?"

"You heard me."

"I heard you, but I don't think I understood you."

He stared at her for several seconds before nodding. "No, you understood, you just don't want to answer the question. Fair enough, you didn't say no right off."

She reached over and touched his arm. "Darius, what exactly are you saying?"

"I'm asking you to marry me, Liz."

She frowned, then looked at her son.

He shook his head. "No, no this is not about Marc. This is about you and me. Of course, having him in my life every day would be perfect, but that is not why I'm asking so don't confuse the matter."

"Then why else?"

His eyes widened as if surprised by the question.

"Because I love you, of course, and I thought—"

"I do," she confirmed quickly. No matter whatever else was said, she would not have him walking away once again believing she felt nothing for him.

"Then what's the problem?"

"We could never have a regular relationship, Darius. Not after everything that has happened."

"How can you…" He paused, leaned closer to her and lowered his voice to a whisper. "How can you sit here and say that after last night?"

Liz folded her arms across her chest and simply stared at him.

"What?" he asked, his brows scrunched in obvious annoyance.

"I'm just amazed. You haven't changed at all. Here

I was worried that you had changed too much, and you haven't changed at all."

One of the thick eyebrows shot up. "Neither have you apparently. You still don't know what the hell you want."

Liz had had enough. She got out of the car and closed her door, but before she could open the door to the back seat to carry Marc back to their bungalow, Darius had gotten out and come around the car.

"You are as controlling as ever!" she hissed at him. "You still think that just because you want something a certain way, it should be that way."

"If it makes sense—why not?!"

"Darius, you can't just expect me to drop everything and move around the world because we were together one night."

"If you had no intention of having a relationship with me then what was last night about?"

Liz said nothing, knowing the truth would only make matters worse.

"Oh, I get it now. While I was making love, you were having sex," he snapped.

Liz didn't say a word, despite the fact that he was far from the truth. She'd wanted only to have sex. She'd fully intended only to have sex. But she now understood that was impossible with Darius. They had too much history, there were too many conflicting memories and too much raw emotion between them ever to just be occasional lovers.

His dark eyes narrowed on her face. "Fine, if that's how you want to play it."

He turned to the car and opened the door quickly, lifting Marc into his arms. Liz followed him through the hotel lobby and out the back toward their bungalow. But with every step his easy capitulation troubled her more and more. By the time they had reached the bungalow she was sure something had gone terribly wrong between them. Once again, their relationship had taken another ineradicable turn.

She used the key to open the door and Darius carried Marc to his bedroom and laid him down. Hearing the commotion Dee came out of her room, with her knitting project still clutched in her hands.

"Oh, you're back."

Liz looked at her aunt, more than a little suspicious of her sudden recovery over the course of a few hours.

"You look much better, Dee," Darius said, coming back into the living room.

"Yes, much better," Liz muttered, her suspicions growing.

"I feel better." She smiled innocently. "Did you all have a good time?"

Darius and Liz looked at each other, but neither answered the question.

"Well, I'd better get going." Darius headed toward the door. "Liz, may I talk to you for a moment?"

Glancing at her aunt, Liz reluctantly followed him out the door. As soon as it was closed behind her he turned on her.

"After your family is asleep, I expect you at my bungalow tonight."

"What are you talking about?"

"Some women can't appreciate love, they only understand being used. I never thought you were one of those woman. But the way you went chasing after Darren like a bitch in heat—"

The cracking sound of flesh connecting with flesh resounded on the air, as they both stood stock-still. Liz was as surprised that she'd slapped him as Darius was to be slapped.

He reached up and touched his tender cheek. "I expect you at my bungalow by midnight—don't be late." He turned and started down the walk.

"Like hell!" she called to his retreating back.

At the end of the walk he turned to her and she saw pure fire and brimstone reflected in his brown eyes. "We have an agreement, remember?"

Liz gasped at the pure disgust that dripped from every word. "That *agreement* is null and void."

He turned away, and for a moment Liz thought he might concede, then he turned back. "You have two choices. At midnight tonight you come to my bungalow, or I come to yours. The choice is up to you." He turned and walked back toward the lobby, never looking back.

# Chapter 16

As Liz reentered the suite her head was still spinning. It always amazed her how quickly good things could go bad.

"What was all that commotion about?" Dee asked, her face showing serious concern, and Liz suspected Dee had heard more than she pretended.

"Nothing, Aunt Dee." Liz went into her bedroom and closed the door. She stretched out across the bed and closed her eyes and finally confronted the truth. Maybe Darius was right. Maybe she just didn't know what she wanted. No, that was not true, because she knew exactly what she wanted. She wanted him. She wanted just what Darius was offering her—a chance to be his wife. Only she could see the handwriting on the wall that apparently he was oblivious to.

She knew that every time a good-looking guest

smiled at her too long, Darius would suspect. She knew that every time she announced an impending pregnancy, Darius would wonder. She knew that every time she was late coming home from work, or was away from him for any length of time, Darius would think back to the last time she did not show up. He would remember it because her betrayal was one of the major events that had shaped his current life. He'd ended up in New Zealand because of her. Was he really so naive as to believe they could just pick up the pieces as if nothing had happened and go on?

Well, she was not so naive. She knew that the most she could ever hope for with Darius was stolen weeks here and there, like the one they were sharing. Or a life of misery, for her at least.

She wiped her eyes on the blanket that no longer smelled like Darius. Housekeeping had come while she was out and taken away all the remnants of their night together. The perfect symbolism, she thought.

All she would ever have were faded memories of Darius, pieces of time that she had no way of holding onto or protecting. Except Marc. She would always have that wonderful, that best part of him no matter whatever else happened between them.

She pulled herself together and went in search of her aunt. She found Dee in her bedroom, sitting knitting in a side chair that she had positioned near the window for best light.

Dee was so involved in her craft Liz realized she went unnoticed, so she leaned against the doorway and just enjoyed being in the presence of the only mother figure in her life anymore.

Several minutes later, Dee glanced up and jumped

slightly. "Oh! You scared me. What are you doing just standing there?"

Liz shrugged. "Just standing here." She came into the room and took a seat on the end of the bed. "What are you making?"

"A sweater for that nice young man that works with Darius. He was so thoughtful today, coming around every hour to check on me. I know he was told to look in on me, but he did a lot more than he had to."

Liz thought about the fact that Alika lived on a tropical island and probably had no need of a sweater, but decided to keep the thought to herself. *Who knows, maybe one day he'll travel.*

"So, what were you and Darius arguing about outside?"

"I think you already know."

Dee shrugged and continued her knitting, but something about the shrug struck Liz as more knowing than not.

"Were you really sick this morning?"

Dee's agile fingers paused over her project and then in a blink they were going once more. "What makes you think I was not?"

"You seemed to have recovered awfully fast considering all the moaning and groaning you were doing this morning."

"Well, dear, everyone heals differently. Those antacid tablets were just what I needed."

"You played sick so Marc and I could have some time alone with Darius, didn't you?"

Dee sighed. "For all the good it did." She frowned at Liz. "Were you two arguing like that all day?"

"No, actually, most of the day was pretty terrific. He took us all over the area. It really is beautiful here."

"So what went wrong?"

"When we got back to the hotel, he asked me to marry him."

Dee's eyes widened. "And what was your answer?"

Liz bit her lip trying to remember the exact sequence of events. "I don't think I did."

"What?"

"Everything kinda fell apart so fast, I don't think I said yes or no." She picked at the blanket, seeking some outlet for her nervous energy. "Although I'm quite sure he believes my answer is no."

"I don't understand. How do you go from marriage proposals one moment to arguments the next?"

Liz shook her head. "I don't know, Aunt Dee. I don't know anything when it comes to this man."

"Do you want to marry him?"

"*Want* has nothing to do with it."

"How did you come to that conclusion?"

Liz tilted her head at her aunt. "Do you honestly think he and I could have anything approaching a normal marriage?"

Dee huffed. "Well, first we'd have to define what a normal marriage is, but that's a conversation for another day. As for you and Darius, I think you can have a good marriage if you both desire to make it so."

"After everything we've been through?"

"Sweetheart." Dee leaned forward in her seat. "You're sitting here with your heart breaking at the thought of not being with him for the rest of your life…after everything you've been through. You're working out the complicated relationship of trying to raise a child together…after everything you've been through. And—" Dee returned her attention to her knitting "—you allowed him back in your bed, the first man in ten years…after everything you've been through." She glanced at Liz and quickly looked away. "So, I don't really see your point."

Liz's mouth twisted in an annoyed expression. *After hearing it put like that neither do I.*

"I just don't want to spend my life living like some kind of rehabilitated cheater."

"Are you sure that's how he would treat you?"

"How could he not? I left him for his brother."

"I think you're making a lot of assumptions." Dee nodded thoughtfully, her busy fingers moving deftly over the yarn. "It's understandable. You're frightened out of your mind, and assuming the worse and avoiding the risk is always easier than the alternative."

"And what's that?"

"Isn't it obvious? Putting your heart in jeopardy. And forgiving yourself."

Later that evening, Darius watched the stairs constantly, expecting Liz to appear for dinner, but when only Dee and Marc arrived he knew he would not be seeing her that evening.

"Hi, Uncle Darius!" Marc charged at him with the same enthusiasm as always, and Darius welcomed the weight of his son as he caught the boy in his arms. If only his mother were able to love and trust so easily, Darius thought.

"Where's Liz?" he asked Dee.

"I think she may have caught what I had," Dee said, trying to infuse just the right amount of sympathy in her voice.

"I see," he said, not knowing what else to say. "Well, I guess it's just us then tonight."

Marc immediately began to squirm to get out of his father's hold. "I see my friends."

Darius dropped him and he took off to the other end of the beach.

"So do I," Dee said as she spotted the McKinseys gesturing for her to join them. "Why don't you join us?" she asked, and he knew it was out of her guilt in abandoning him.

"No, I've got too much to do, but thanks anyway." Darius spent most of the evening moving among the guests and answering questions about the surrounding area's attractions and activities.

He kept looking up the stairs hoping to see Liz at the top, but by ten-thirty he knew she would not be coming. He'd threatened to go to her, but he wasn't at all sure he could do that. It would be too painful to make love to her—for that was all he knew how to do when it came to Liz—knowing she didn't feel the same.

He found an empty table and took a seat. That was the most confusing part of all because he was almost certain she loved him, too. So, what exactly was the hang-up? What did she mean when she said he didn't trust her? He wouldn't have asked her to be his wife if he didn't trust her.

What did she want from him? He was tempted to climb the stairs and ask her directly.

Just then Dee appeared at his side. "Darius, have you seen Marc? I haven't seen him in the last hour."

Darius looked around the group and realized the group of children Marc had been playing with were all missing. Wherever they were, they were together and there was some small comfort in that.

"Don't worry, I'll find him."

Darius notified his security staff of the missing children. He and the others split in different directions. One went west down the beach, the other went east up the beach and Darius took the stairs going up to check the hotel complex.

He searched all the nooks and crannies he knew were catnip to the children of his guests. He tried to stay calm, tried to tell himself they were children and probably just off somewhere making that mischief his mother had insisted he never made. But it was hard when all he could think about was how close he'd come to not even knowing Marc, and then almost losing him.

Darius knew nothing in the world was guaranteed, not even the life of a nine-year-old boy. In the lobby, he picked up one of the walkie-talkies so he could communicate with the other two searchers. Both men checked in and neither had found any of the children.

Darius was already considering what to do next. He would have to tell Liz and then call in the local authorities. He started out toward the front lobby door when he noticed a group of lumpy shadows in the back of the lobby where a group of chairs had been pushed together around a table.

As he approached the group, he knew at once it was the missing children. First he breathed a sigh of relief, then he notified security and asked one of the guards to let Dee know Marc was okay.

The kids were all huddled together around a small side table, and they all seemed completely engrossed by whatever was going on on the table. He was close enough now to see that Marc was in the center of the group with a small colorful rag in his hand. The children were all staring at the rag while Marc tried to pour water over it.

Then the rag moved, shivering and releasing a pitiful chirp, and Darius discovered to his amazement the colorful rag was actually an injured bird. "Marc, what are you doing?"

The children jumped in collective startled surprise as Marc turned tearful eyes up to his father. "He's going to die and I don't know how to save him." He lifted his bundle up to Darius. "You gotta help him, Uncle Darius, or he'll die." His little face was completely coated in his misery, as his eyes poured tears and his nose ran uncontrollably.

The other children just watched in their own sorrowful way. None seemed to be taking it as hard as Marc, but it was quite obvious they were all concerned for the bird.

Looking down at the helpless animal, Darius felt helpless himself. He had no idea what to do for an injured wild bird. But, he decided, it was times like this when it was good to have a little pull.

As gently as he could, Darius took the tiny, fragile thing from his son's hands, amazed that Marc had not crushed it by accident. He quickly walked to the lobby desk with the entourage of children following, and was more than relieved to see it was Alika behind the desk.

"Alika, I need something to put this in."

Alika frowned down at the dying bird. "What is that?"

"Just give me a box or something!"

Alika reached beneath the counter and emptied a small cardboard box they used to hold lost and found keys and other odd items.

"Punch some small holes in the top of it," Darius said as Alika attempted to give him the box.

After the holes were in place, Darius gently lowered the animal into the box. "Okay, now I need you to help me find a twenty-four-hour vet clinic in the area."

"Boss, I don't know if such a thing exists."

"Just look it up on the Internet, Alika. There has to be at least one pet hospital in this area."

Alika's eyes widened as he looked at the computer screen. "Uh, no pet hospital in this area, but there is one in Christchurch and the doctor who owns it is named Elton McGillicutty."

"A vet in Christchurch is not going to help this bird, Alika! Find something local!"

"Boss, what I'm saying is that we have a Dr. Elton McGillicutty staying with us this week. How many Dr. Elton McGillicuttys can there be in New Zealand?"

If he weren't holding a half-dead bird in a box, Darius thought he just might kiss Alika at that moment. "Where is his bungalow?"

"He's in the Karora suite."

"Great, I'm headed there. Call down to the beach and ask security to check the guests at dinner and see if he's there as well. And after that, call the suite and see if anyone answers."

Darius, holding his box as if it were precious diamonds, moved to the doors leading to the back entrance. By now he had lost some of the watching children but many of them followed Marc, who followed Darius down and around the winding paths.

Soon they were knocking on the door and it was quickly opened by an elderly, gray-haired man whose eyes went immediately to the box. "I understand you have a patient for me."

As Darius entered the suite, he saw that the doctor had already laid out a cloth and his instruments on a small writing table. "Do you know what happened to him?" Dr. McGillicutty asked.

Darius gently placed the small box on the table. "I have no idea, but if you can save him, Doc, you can stay at my hotel free for the rest of your life."

Dr. McGillicutty smiled and his eyes widened. "Well now, that's as good a motivation as I've ever had."

Darius shooed the children back out of the suite as a startled Mrs. McGillicutty was coming out of the bathroom. She'd obviously just taken a shower, and Darius apologized for the interruption.

"Doc, I'll be right out here when you're done," Darius said, pulling the door closed.

He and Marc went to a nearby tree and propped themselves against it, as the other children eventually wandered off to find other entertainment.

Marc's small face was as solemn and serious as Darius had ever seen him. "I'm sure the doctor knows what he's doing, Marc."

"I know." He nodded thoughtfully.

"So what's wrong?"

"I was just wondering, what if he needed a kidney? His daddy is not around to give him one like mine was. I don't want him to die because he needs a kidney."

Darius's heart had stopped beating at the words *like mine was*. He swallowed hard. "Marc, do you believe I'm your father?"

Marc looked up at him, slightly confused. "Aren't you?"

"Well, yes, but—" Darius felt as though he was wading into some pretty deep water, but he didn't know if he should turn around or keep going. "How did you know I was your father?"

"You gave me a perfect kidney."

Darius frowned. "That's it?"

Marc nodded. "Who else could do that?"

Darius might have informed him that anyone with the right blood and genetic makeup could have, but he wasn't about to spoil this perfect gift. "Then why do you still call me Uncle Darius?"

"That's what Mom told me to call you."

Darius blinked and waited. He blinked again, realizing that that was all the answer that would be forthcoming. *Out of the mouths of babes,* he thought.

"You think he'll need a kidney?" Marc's small, round face looked up at Darius with such earnestness, Darius only wished life and death were within his power. In that moment, he would've given half his hotel to save the life of that little bird.

"No, I don't think he needs a kidney. I think his wing is a little hurt, and the doc will fix him up just fine."

Just then, the door opened and Elton McGillicutty came out with a soft smile on his face, wiping his hands on a dark-colored cloth. "Well, I believe with a little time our patient will be flying once more."

"Yeah!" Marc jumped up and down and then rushed to hug the doctor. "That you, Dr. Mickinaniny, thank you so much."

The doctor smiled at Darius, and ran his hand over Marc's short hair. "No problem at all. I'll just keep him here over the next few days if that's okay with you."

"Can I come by and see him sometime?" Marc beamed up at the doctor and then at his father looking as though the weight of the world had been lifted off his shoulders.

"Marc, we don't want to bother the doc—"

Dr. McGillicutty lifted his hand. "It's no problem at all. If we happen to be in the room he's perfectly welcome to drop by."

Darius reached forward and shook the doctor's hand. "Thank you so much, sir. You have no idea how grateful I truly am."

Dr. McGillicutty took the handshake and leaned forward slightly. "Did you mean what you said earlier?"

"Absolutely. In fact, this trip is on me. Just stop by the check-out desk when you get ready to leave and we'll reverse the charges."

He and Marc started to walk away. "Thanks again." Marc waved back.

As he led his son back to his suite, he found that there was so much he wanted to say, but he thought he should first talk to Liz. They arrived on the main path at the same time as Dee and the McKinseys were coming up from the beach, and instead of going all the way to their bungalow, he said his goodnights to them there on the path and headed back to his own suite. It was almost midnight and he had an appointment.

## Chapter 17

Darius quickly prepared his suite. The bottle of champagne he'd ordered was sitting on the table on ice, already chilling. He went into the bedroom and took a quick shower and dressed in black silk pajamas.

Even as he laid out the matching silk negligee, Darius knew there was a more than fifty-fifty chance Liz would not appear tonight. As for going to her, Darius wasn't sure what he would do. He knew there was a part of him that could not resist such a challenge, but another part did not want to cause her even one more second of unhappiness at his hands.

He waited by the front window that overlooked the harbor, watching as the staff cleaned up the remains of the evening's dinner. It was two minutes after midnight when he heard the soft tapping on the door.

Something in his chest instantly uncoiled and he

moved across the room to answer. She stood on the threshold with a solemn expression and a determined glint in her eyes, and Darius knew that despite her willingness to come tonight he was still in for a fight.

Without acknowledging his existence, she walked past him and into the suite. "We need to talk."

He closed the door and locked it. "No, we don't. What we're doing doesn't require conversation. That's for lovers, we're just sex buddies, remember?"

She spun around and her narrowed eyes were almost reddish gold. He was instantly hard. Nothing got him hotter faster than a pissed-off Liz.

She closed her eyes and took a deep breath, and then another and he watched fascinated as she tried to rein in her anger. He wondered if she knew she was fighting a losing battle. She lifted her arms in some sort of meditative motion, and he could only shake his head.

Slowly her lids lifted and he saw her eyes had returned to their natural soft brown. *Oh, well,* he thought, *there's more than one way to tick off an ex.*

"Darius, I came here tonight to tell you that I love you."

He tilted his head, caught off guard by the confession.

"I love you and I would love nothing more than to spend my life with you."

Darius's face spread in a wide smile, he couldn't believe what he was hearing. "So, you'll marry me?"

"On one condition."

"Aw, hell." He covered his face with both hands. "I can't believe I let you sucker-punch me again. When will I learn?"

"Just listen! I meant every word I said, I just need to know you trust me. That you can trust me as your wife and partner. I can't go into a marriage thinking that you're always going to be worried about me running off with a first cousin or something!"

"I trust you." *Besides, I don't have any first cousins,* he thought, but wisely kept the thought to himself.

"No, you say that and may even believe it until something happens and then all bets are off."

"So, what do you want me to do, Liz? Take a lie detector test?"

"In a way."

His mouth fell open. "What?"

"Except the lie was not told by you, it was told by me, and I need you to detect it."

He stood on the opposite side of the room just staring at her for several minutes. Then he turned and headed for the bar in the corner. "I need a drink."

He could hear Liz taking another deep breath behind him and he briefly wondered if she were doing her meditation thing again. He considered simply saying something to get her riled beyond return, picking her up, carrying her to the bedroom and having all the wild, animalistic sex either of them could handle. But the problem was that the sun would eventually come up, and she would be even further out of his reach than she was right now.

He poured a brandy and turned to face her again. He took a sip, studying her determined expression over the top of the glass. "Okay, I'm listening."

She nodded. "There is an *untruth* between us."

He frowned. "What kind of *untruth?*"

"Not a lie exactly, just a truth I never shared with you."

He took another sip, and grudgingly admitted to some interest in what she was saying. "And you think this truth is important to our relationship."

"Yes."

"Why?"

"Because it's the only way I can prove to you how much I love you."

"Liz, you don't have to—"

"Yes, I do, Darius. I need you to know this, but you have to know it on a deeper level than me just telling you."

"This is crazy." He shook his head. "So now I'm supposed to play twenty questions with some tidbit about you that I don't even know? How am I ever supposed to figure this out? Up until a few months ago I hadn't seen you in almost ten years! It could be anything!"

She shook her head slowly. "No, not anything. Something you should know. Something the man who loves me *would* know."

"Oh, okay I get it." He took another sip of the brandy. "So, this is not about you proving your love for me at all—it's about me proving my love for you. You're talking in riddles."

"I know. But I don't know how else to explain myself without just coming out and saying what I need you to know!"

"How long do I have to solve this riddle?"

She smiled, a soft sad smile. "As long as you need."

He huffed. "Why should the time frame be any more definitive than the question itself?" He set the brandy glass back down on the bar. "So, just so I have it straight. There is something about you that you've never told me. Something important. Something I should've guessed already, I assume. And you won't marry me unless I can figure out what that *what* is?"

She grinned brightly. "Nicely done."

"Now what?"

She crossed the room to him, and pressed her lips to

his. "Now, we enjoy what time we have together while we have it."

He wrapped his arms around her waist to hold her to him. "Um, I'm all for that but there is something I should tell you first."

"What?"

"Marc knows I'm his father."

"What? How could you? I told you I would tell him in my own time, in my own way! You had no right!"

"I didn't tell him!"

"Then who—" She shook her head against the thought as soon as it formed in her brain. "No, Dee would never—"

"Liz! He guessed on his own."

"What? How?"

"According to him, only a daddy could give a son a perfect kidney."

She frowned in confusion. "But...but he calls you Uncle Darius."

"Yeah, because you told him to."

"Huh?"

"The point is, he knows the truth, apparently has for some time. I think we just need to sit him down tomorrow and talk to him together. Okay?"

She nodded, but the confused expression on her face told him she was still trying to work out the logic of a nine year old in her head. *Good luck with that.*

He gave her a quick peck. "Now that that is out of the way, what were you saying before? Ah yes, let's enjoy the time we have." Without warning, he bent and swooped her up in his arms and carried her into his bedroom.

She reached up and touched his face. "As I was

putting Marc to bed this evening he told me about the bird. Thank you."

"Don't thank me, thank Dr. McGillicutty."

He dropped her unceremoniously on the bed, and before she could bounce back up he was over her, straddling her body. Looking down at her, he said "No matter what you are telling yourself are good enough reasons for us to be apart, I do love you and I know you love me. And we have a child together, and a common history which are all good reasons why we should be together."

"But not enough."

He huffed loudly. "I can't believe my whole future hinges on a damn riddle."

"You'll figure it out." She took his face between her hands and looked directly into his eyes. "All you have to do is pay attention."

Shifting her body, Liz wrapped her legs around his waist and Darius willingly lowered himself on top of her. "Oh, wait." He stood and crossed the room to pick up the negligee he'd bought her. "I kinda wanted to see you in this." He held it up.

Liz sat up on her elbows looking at the flimsy piece of material before climbing to her knees. She reached down and pulled her blouse over her head, bringing her bra along with it. "I thought you wanted to see me in this."

Darius's eyes immediately fixed on her bare breasts, sitting so high and proud. He tossed the negligee back over his shoulder, and headed back to the bed. "You're right, as always."

Stopping beside the bed, he lifted her beneath the arms until her breasts were directly in front of his face. He took one in his mouth and suckled until Liz thought she would cry out, only to switch to the other and repeat the action.

Liz could only brace herself on his shoulders as she tried to slow the quickly building need in her body. With a single touch he could electrify her whole being, and she had yet to find a way to hold out.

Darius stopped momentarily to remove his own clothes, and when she attempted to remove her jeans as well, his large hand came over hers. "Let me."

He quickly disrobed, but took his time removing her clothes. He gently pushed her back against the bed, as he slid his hand over the button-front fly of her jeans. He let his palm flatten over her tummy and she twisted and almost purred for him.

Darius decided that one day he would get her to purr if it took all night. Opening the fly, button by slow button he simply enjoyed the exposure of her bronze skin as it was revealed to him. He came to the top of her black thong panties and stopped.

Looking up at her face he could see she was already halfway there. Sliding his index finger into the top of her panties he found the slit in her body moist with readiness for him. With his other hand, he reached into the nightstand and pulled out a condom, laying on the bed next to her.

He leaned down and whispered at her ear. "Does anybody else make you feel this way, baby?"

Her head turned left and right as she struggled to maintain some connection with reality. "No, nobody, Darius, no one but you. Only you."

Pushing his finger further up inside her, he listened to the soft whimper that escaped her lips, lips that were begging to be kissed, so he did.

Leaning forward he kissed her with all the passion he felt in his heart even as he added another finger inside her. Her hands came up to grip his shoulders and she clung to him as though he was the last lifeboat on a sinking ship.

Darius wanted to bring her to the point of climax with just his fingers, but he doubted he would last that long. Moving back, he pulled her jeans and panties off the rest of the way and in the same way and same motion quickly covered himself with the condom and came over the top of her. "You make me crazy, you know that?" he whispered in her ear as he entered her body.

One again he was surprised by the tightness of her opening. Holding her hips in his large hands he shifted and with one hard thrust drove himself deep inside her. Her small teeth clamped down on his shoulder as a moan came from her throat. "Damn." He hissed at the sweet pain.

She lifted her legs higher and he knew what she wanted. He'd been right before—they didn't need words. What they said to each other was communicated on a deeper level. That's how he knew she still wanted him. How he knew almost instantly that Marc was his. There was something between them, something rare. Something once-in-a-lifetime, and despite her doubts and silly riddles he had no intention of ever letting her go again. They had already lost too many years on things that didn't matter.

Holding her against his chest like the precious thing that she was, he settled into a steady rhythm. She was the mother of his son, the mother of his future children. His first love and the last face he wanted to see before he left this world. She was everything, and whether she ever said the words Darius knew in his heart she felt the same.

He sensed it in her touch, in the way she completely

surrendered her body to him as if she were his and only his, never to be touched by another. Suddenly he stopped in mid stroke as if a veil had been lifted from his eyes.

Braced on his elbows he stared down into her face, a face filled with love and trust. They'd both been so young ten years ago, and although they'd loved each other, mistakes had been made on both sides. They'd both made some bad choices, but some choices were not really choices at all. Some things were known and felt at a bone-deep level that might never be fully understood. *How the hell did I miss that?*

"What?" She was looking up at him slightly confused, slightly annoyed that he'd stopped and all he could do was grin down at her.

He slid forward into her body, and she sighed in relief. *….nobody, Darius, no one but you. Only you.* With precision he slowly pulled out of her body, once more bracing himself over her.

She was still looking up at him, as if waiting, hoping he knew what he now knew. It made sense now. Why this was so important to her, why he needed to realize it on his own. Suddenly everything fell into place. "I solved the riddle."

Her eyes narrowed doubtfully. "Did you?"

She didn't believe him. He was honestly torn between the need to gloat over the fact that this woman was his and his alone, and the need to thrust into her body. Darren had never touched her. Whatever had happened between them, he knew as certainly as he knew his own name that she'd never been with another man. That was why she always felt like his whenever he touched her, because she was.

"Please, Darius, I neeḋ you." With another soft

whimper, she lifted her upper body bringing her breast right to his mouth as if it were a gift, and he decided he could always gloat later. Darius took one of the breasts into his mouth, marveling that even her breasts were the perfect size.

Holding her tight against his chest he pushed into her body until the need overcame both of them, and he felt her arrive at their destination first. As her hot juices rained down on him, unable to hold back any longer, Darius followed her over the edge of the cliff into the abyss, into paradise.

# *Epilogue*

"Uncle Darius! Look!" Marc lifted his fishing pole to reveal he had once again lost his bait. "Where did it go?"

"The fish ate it, son."

His brow, so like his father's crinkled in confusion. "That's not fair."

"Not fair at all," he agreed as he retied another small piece of bait to the line.

On the other side of the lake, Liz wasn't having any better luck. "Darius!"

He turned to see his new wife looking at the tree overhead. He followed her line of vision and realized her pole had gotten tangled in the tree. He glanced back to where Dee sat beneath the shade of an umbrella.

"Whose idea was it again to teach them how to fish?"

Dee continued with her knitting, her deft fingers never missing a stroke. "Yours, I believe."

"Next time I get any bright ideas, Dee, you have to try and talk me out of them."

"I'll try." She continued knitting away as Darius waded across the pond to help Liz get her pole out of the tree.

As he approached, she smiled sheepishly. "Sorry, I guess my backstroke is more powerful than I realized."

"This is fishing, Liz, you're not suppose to have a backstroke—that's swimming."

"Well, whatever it is, it's up in that tree."

He shook his head. "Here, take this one for now," he said, handing her his perfect pole and secretly wondering if he'd ever see it again in that condition.

She stood with her hand on her hip watching him. Even dressed in hip waders and one of his old baseball caps she was the sexiest thing he'd ever seen.

"Ever miss your carefree bachelor days?" she asked, watching as he attempted to detangle the pole in the tree.

"Not for a moment," he answered without hesitation. "I only wish we had married sooner. My son would be a decent fisherman by now." He glanced at her over his shoulder. "And he wouldn't be calling me Uncle Darius."

"I told you, I think it's just like a pet name. He'll grow out of it eventually."

"I hope so, otherwise, it might make teacher conferences and the like a bit awkward. Stop watching me and practice your stroke," he grumbled.

His grumble was met by a slight snicker, but she did turn back and throw her line to the water. "I forgot to tell you, I got a call from one of the schools I applied to, I have an interview on Monday."

"That's great."

"It would be great if I actually get the job."

"If you don't you can always work at the hotel with me, or not work at all. I have every intention of keeping you barefoot and pregnant anyway."

"We've only been married a couple of months…pace yourself." She chuckled.

"Marc needs a sibling before he gets too old."

"Are you serious, Darius?" She asked the question quietly, and Darius knew how important the answer would be.

"I would love to have a child right away, but if you're not ready that's okay, too."

She wiped her forehead in an exaggerated gesture. "Whew, that's good because I didn't know if the mailman would accept this baby."

Darius stopped pulling at the fishing line as her words sank in. "Liz, are you trying to tell me in your own twisted little way that you're pregnant?"

She glanced at him with a satisfied smile and looked away. "Maybe."

"Don't play with me, woman, are you pregnant or not?" He climbed down from the tree in half the time it had taken him to climb it.

She dropped the line and turned to him and he could see then how hard it had been for her to hold it in this long. "Yes! Yes! I'm pregnant!"

Darius lifted her in his arms and swung her around, not believing how his whole world had turned around in the past year. He knew he was blessed beyond reason, and doubly blessed if you considered how close he'd come to losing a chance to be a part of this family. The family that was always meant to be his. The woman that could *only* be his.

"Hey, guys!" Darius called to Dee and Marc across the lake. "We're pregnant!"

Dee dropped her knitting, but Marc didn't seem overly impressed.

"Pregnant?" Dee called back. "Oh, how wonderful."

"Congratulations!" another fisherman called from downstream, and Darius suddenly remembered they were not alone on the small lake.

"Yeah, congrats!" someone called from the other direction.

"Thank you!" he called to both.

"When are you due?" Dee called across the lake.

"I'm not sure yet, I have an appointment with the doctor tomorrow!" Liz called back.

"Mom! Aunt Dee! You're scaring off all the fish!" Marc called from the rock he was perched on.

"Sorry, sweetheart," Liz called back before realizing what she was doing. "Oops," she whispered to Darius.

Darius was simply staring at her with all the love in his heart. "You make me very happy, you always have."

She reached up on tiptoes and kissed his lips. "The same goes for me." She smiled. "It just took me a little longer to appreciate it." She laid her head against his shoulder. "Are you really happy about the baby?"

Darius shifted their bodies until they were both facing Marc who was now bent over the lake looking for something in the water. Darius assumed it was probably his last piece of bait.

"Just promise to give me another one of those, and for the record the female version is just fine with me."

"Thank you," she said softly.

"For what?"

Liz gestured to the surroundings. "For making this paradise your home, our home. For giving our son a second chance at life." She chuckled. "And for letting me bring Aunt Dee along when we moved here."

"First of all, I would've insisted you bring Dee. What

were we supposed to do? Leave her to those barracudas in Cincinnati? Second of all, although it's a roundabout way why you're the reason I ended up here, in a way you picked this home, I didn't. And finally, instead of thanking me for giving my son a kidney, how about I thank you for giving me a son?"

Liz smiled to herself, content in the knowledge that despite all the bad choices she made, fate would not, *could not* be denied. They were both older and much changed by life, but their shared destiny had finally been fulfilled. Through it all, their love had survived.

Somehow, just knowing that, Liz was able to release the heavy guilt she'd carried for so long. She had betrayed the man she loved, and kept his son a secret for almost ten years, but the love shining in his eyes as he looked up at her at that moment was a balm to her battered soul. He loved her. He forgave her…because love forgives all. And it was because of that certainty that Liz was able to forgive herself.

She lifted her lips to his and he kissed her gently and then with more passion until both of them had forgotten where they were. They were both brought back to reality at the sound of a heavy splash in the water.

They looked up to see Marc standing up in the water, dripping wet from head to toe, a wide grin on his mouth as he lifted the result of his wild dive. A tiny sardine squirmed at the end of his pole.

"You know," Darius said, pulling his pregnant wife back against his chest, "my son just might make a fine fisherman after all."

\* \* \* \* \*

# REQUEST YOUR FREE BOOKS!

## 2 FREE NOVELS
## PLUS 2 FREE GIFTS!

**KIMANI ROMANCE**

### Love's ultimate destination!

# HELP CELEBRATE ARABESQUE'S 15TH ANNIVERSARY!

## 2009 marks Arabesque's 15th anniversary!

Help us celebrate by telling us about your most special memories and moments with Arabesque books. Entries will be judged by the Arabesque Anniversary Committee based on which are the most touching and well written. Fifteen lucky winners will receive as a prize a full-grain leather duffel bag with the Arabesque anniversary logo.